UNTIL IT HURTS TO STOP

UNTIL IT
HURTS
TO STOP

JENNIFER R. HUBBARD
AUTHOR OF *THE SECRET YEAR* AND *TRY NOT TO BREATHE*

VIKING
An Imprint of Penguin Group (USA) Inc.

VIKING
Published by the Penguin Group
Penguin Group (USA) Inc.
375 Hudson Street
New York, New York 10014, U.S.A.

USA / Canada / UK / Ireland / Australia / New Zealand / India / South Africa / China
Penguin Books Ltd, Registered Offices: 80 Strand, London WC2R 0RL, England

For more information about the Penguin Group visit www.penguin.com

First published in the United States of America by Viking, an imprint of Penguin Group
(USA) Inc., 2013

LIBRARY OF CONGRESS CATALOGING-IN-PUBLICATION DATA
Hubbard, Jennifer R.
Until it hurts to stop / by Jennifer R. Hubbard.
pages cm
Summary: A former victim of middle school bullying, seventeen-year-old Maggie
struggles to navigate the high school world of love and friendships, finding solace in
her love of hiking.
ISBN 978-0-670-78520-9 (hardcover)
[1. Self-acceptance—Fiction. 2. Bullying—Fiction. 3. Interpersonal relations—Fiction.
4. Hiking—Fiction. 5. High schools—Fiction. 6. Schools—Fiction.] I. Title.
PZ7.H8582Un 2013
[Fic]—dc23
2013012795

Printed in USA

10 9 8 7 6 5 4 3 2 1

Designed by Eileen Savage
Set in Dante

PEARSON

UNTIL IT HURTS TO STOP

My friend Nick reaches across the cafeteria table and drops a knife into my hand. "Happy birthday, Maggie."

I turn the knife over in my hand. I have always wanted one of these. I've borrowed Nick's often enough, out on the trails.

I know I should hide it. It's a Swiss army knife, not a weapon, but our school gets hysterical over nail clippers. They'd probably confiscate it and put me on some list of budding terrorists.

Even so, I can't resist stroking the smooth metal and snapping open the different tools: the nail file, the screwdriver, the tiny scissors. Best of all, I love the tiny scissors. Nobody else is near enough to see me handling this supposed instrument of danger, anyway. Nick's legs sprawl into the space next to him, discouraging anyone from sitting too close.

"Thank you." I give the knife a last squeeze and slip it into my pocket. "It'll be perfect for our next hike."

Nick's stepfather, Perry, first brought us onto the trails when we were fourteen. Now that Perry's knees are shot and Nick has a driver's license, Nick and I hike alone.

"About that," Nick says, winding spaghetti around his fork. "I thought we could try your suggestion."

"What suggestion?"

"To climb a mountain."

"What? When did I say that?"

"When we were at Silver Creek."

"Oh, right." We'd hiked in Silver Creek State Park a couple of weeks ago, just before school started. After slogging through the park, crossing about a dozen streams (balancing on stones, teetering on slippery logs), we'd finally reached a hilltop with a view of the Porte Range to our south. Glowing with success—or endorphins—I'd said, waving at the mountains, "I bet the view's even better from up there."

"Now there's an idea," Nick had said.

And I, who was normally afraid of—well, pretty much everything—had laughed with excitement. Nick and I have hiked some hills, but never any real mountains. Yet in that moment, I believed I could climb anything.

The mountains looked like home—some long-forgotten home—and they looked tough. Sharp-toothed, with a dangerous beauty. Gray and lilac and blue. They loomed on the horizon, silent and immense. Nick and I stared at them, their quiet power sinking into our bones, until mosquitoes and a race with the setting sun drove us back onto the Silver Creek trail. And I put mountains out of my mind.

Until now.

"I can't believe you're bringing that up," I say. "I wasn't serious." Except maybe for a moment.

"We could *get* serious about it," Nick says. "How about Eagle Mountain?"

"The one Perry climbed?"

"Yeah."

Nick says it like he's offering me my own private island and a vault full of gold. A picture of Perry grinning on Eagle's summit hangs in the downstairs hall of their house. I tell myself it can't have been *too* bad a climb if he was able to smile like that. Still— "I'm not sure I can make it up a mountain."

"I'm not sure I can either," Nick says, "but let's find out."

I rub a smear of mustard off the crust of my sandwich, turning over the idea in my mind. "This isn't going to be like Mount Everest, is it? Where if you can't make it, they leave you in the snow to die?"

Nick laughs. "Eagle's not even a mile high. But if it helps, Maggie—I promise I won't leave you in the snow to die."

"How do you know *I* won't leave *you* in the snow?"

"Because I'll have the car keys. Besides, there is no snow around here in September."

The plan makes my mouth water, despite the prickling in my nerves. Sometimes the best hikes were when Perry, Nick, and I tested ourselves, like when we hiked farther than I thought I could, or faced extreme weather. I remember the sparkle of crusted snow on a subzero day, and the ice formations we saw at Hemlock Brook—pillars and palaces seen by nobody else, as the printless snow around us proved. Even though the air stung my throat, I managed to keep myself from freezing; I pushed myself out into a day when most people stayed home.

Remembering the surge of power, the sense of belonging, that I felt at Hemlock Brook and at Silver Creek, I want to feel it again.

"Okay," I say. I wish I could flick open my knife to accept the challenge. "To the mountains!" I could cry, but you need to be brandishing a sword to carry that off—and possibly sitting on a horse. An Excalibur-type flourish might be too dramatic for my little blade, but I like the symbolism, and it would get a laugh out of Nick. I would do it if I didn't have to worry about the teachers patrolling the lunchroom.

"Saturday?"

"Sure. But remember, nobody leaves anyone in the snow," I say as my friend Sylvie takes the seat next to me.

"Snow? What snow?" she asks, biting into a pear.

"Never mind." I touch the chain around my neck. "Listen, thank you for the necklace."

Sylvie slipped me her present in the hall after third period, since we don't have any classes together. I've been wearing it ever since. It's a necklace with a stone the same emerald color as peacock feathers.

"Oh, do you like it? It's malachite. I thought the color would be perfect for you."

"I love it." While she returns to her pear, I say, "Why are you here? I thought you had a yearbook committee meeting. Or something." I can never keep Sylvie's committees, clubs, and teams straight. Her calendar is a blur of plans and appointments. We can barely get through a conversation without some reminder or incoming message beeping at her.

"I did. And it went on forever. I wouldn't even be getting *this* much to eat if this girl, Raleigh, hadn't taken over." Sylvie laughs. "It was her first meeting, but she practically ran the whole thing. Not that I'm complaining. Because otherwise, we'd still be there, debating whether to put the sports-team pictures before or after the student council pictures."

"Raleigh?" I repeat, my stomach beginning to burn. I know only one person with that name. "Raleigh Barringer? She's back?"

"'Back'? Oh, right . . . She did say she used to live here. Before I moved in."

"She went to West End Junior High," I say through numb lips. "With me."

Nick looks up from his spaghetti.

"Well, she said her family's been living in Italy for two years." Sylvie scrolls through one of her endless to-do lists. "Nick, did you do the math homework yet?"

While Sylvie eats and chats with Nick, my ears buzz. I swear I can taste stomach acid.

Raleigh Barringer.

I thought I would never see her again. I'd celebrated her move to Italy the way people cheer the toppling of maniacal dictators.

And before I can recover from hearing her name again, I hear her voice, screeching somewhere behind me. Her laugh is a cold fingernail ripping my skin open, right down the back of my neck.

It paralyzes me. For a minute all I can do is watch Nick slide bread over his sauce-covered plate. He keeps glancing at me, but I won't meet his eyes. I have to be in mental lockdown, all my energy focused inward. Because otherwise the panic flashing through me might burst out, right in the middle of the cafeteria, for everyone to see.

two

At the end of lunch, I escape to the girls' room, where I check under the stalls for feet. I pick the stall farthest from everyone else, double-check the bolt, and stand with my eyes closed. *Raleigh Barringer. What the hell is she doing back here? And what is she going to do to me this time?*

Toilets flush; girls talk and laugh; faucets run. All of it echoes off the cold olive tile, ringing against my skull.

I need to think, to get myself together. I might run into Raleigh in the hallway at any moment. If I'm really unlucky, I might meet her at the sinks in a few seconds. I have to know what to say, how to act.

The bathroom door thumps hollowly, and I check to make sure all the feet have left. The emptying of the room means the bell's about to ring.

I'm out of time.

I dash out the door and through the halls, ears tuned to what's happening on all sides of me. But I never look at faces, never risk eye contact. I slip through the door of my French class as the bell sounds.

In French, I sit next to Vanessa Webb. Today she's in crisp white, which would make me look like a hepatitis case. (Sylvie says I should wear "jewel tones," whatever those are.)

Vanessa recites the day's lesson, a story about a guy named Jean-Claude buying bread at the *boulangerie*. The people in our French book never do anything exciting like fight tigers or shoot white-water rapids. Although Vanessa reads with an actress's animation and timing, half the class nods off. I play with my pen cap, which I've gnawed until it's white and frayed around the edges. For the four thousandth time, I vow to stop chewing my pen cap.

But I can't even keep that resolution till the end of class. While Vanessa narrates Jean-Claude's culinary adventures, my mind returns to Raleigh Barringer—definitely the worst birthday gift of all. And I find myself biting the plastic cap again, working it with my teeth.

Bio is my last class of the day. The teacher, Mr. Thornhart, is discombobulated because the guys in the back of the room have been throwing around stray worm parts during the dissection labs. And so he's decided to reshuffle the lab partners, pairing up everyone himself. He's like some deranged matchmaker who hasn't bothered to find out our most basic traits, except which of us are more likely than others to use worm parts as projectiles.

"Margaret Camden and Adriana Lippold." He taps the table where we're supposed to sit.

Adriana and I both freeze. Then she takes her seat, keeping her eyes on the lab bench.

"Margaret? Did you hear me?" Thornhart asks.

I consider not moving. I would rather stick my hand in a toaster than work with the girl who was Raleigh Barringer's best friend back in junior high—and still is, for all I know. I may be a year older today, but the world seems to be doing its best to stuff me back into eighth grade.

Thornhart's already moving on, announcing the next happy couple. I grab my books and edge into the seat next to Adriana, not looking at her.

"I can't believe he put us together," she mutters.

I grunt.

"You don't have to act like it's such a burden to you, though," she goes on. "I'm sure I can find my way around a worm as well as you can."

I tighten my fingers around my pen. *What does she mean by that? "As well as you can," in that vinegar voice of hers?* I raise an eyebrow at her and let her interpret that any way she wants.

We take turns at the microscope, exchanging the slides we've already viewed for the ones we haven't, silence thick between us. I sneak glances at Adriana, trying to gauge the danger. She has plucked her eyebrows in a high, arched shape, so they swoop across her forehead like bird wings. Her lipstick is pale pink—an innocent, harmless color.

But that pale-pink mouth is the same one that sneered at me back in junior high, that said I was ugly, that any boy would puke rather than touch me. It's the same mouth that laughed when Raleigh Barringer said I should hang myself, because nobody wanted me at school where I could turn the stomachs of normal people.

Adriana and I say nothing to each other now. The glass slides scrape the benchtop as we pass them back and forth. And I wonder if Thornhart has any clue what a spectacularly bad idea it was to put us together.

three

A fter school, Luis Morales and I sit in Nick's car, waiting for Nick to start the engine. This takes a while, because Nick is plowing through layers of dirty clothes and empty cracker boxes on the floor to find a half-full bag of chocolate chip cookies he remembers stashing there at some point. I slip my hand into my pocket and stroke the sleek surface of my new knife, wishing it had a cookie locator—maybe in between the screwdriver and the nail file. All I want is to get off school grounds, to put as much distance as possible between Raleigh Barringer and myself. "Nick, it's a ten-minute ride. You can't drop us off first and *then* hunt for your cookies?"

"Hey, I want some cookies, too," Luis says.

"What the hell is this?" Nick holds up a shard of plastic.

"You sure it wasn't holding the car together?" Luis says, laughing.

Nick tosses it onto the backseat next to me, and follows it

with a hat I don't remember ever seeing him wearing. I hope there are no jockstraps buried in the mess.

The car doesn't smell nearly as bad as you might expect, given how much junk is piled in here. I suppose everything's been here so long, it has all dried out. Like the petrified French fry on the floor at my feet. (At least I'm pretty sure it's a French fry.)

"I'd like to get out of here before it's time to climb Eagle," I say.

"Climb Eagle?" Luis asks. "What do you want to do that for?"

"For fun," Nick says. We would invite Luis to hike with us—have invited him, in fact—but Luis would rather stick needles in his eyes. He doesn't see the point of trekking out into the woods, where there isn't even a store or a coffee shop or any music. The vacant lot near school is enough of a wilderness for him.

"Found 'em!" Nick pulls out a crumpled bag and peers inside. "Yeah, still some left." He holds out the bag. "You first, Maggie. Since it's your birthday and all."

"It's your birthday?" Luis says. "Hey, happy birthday, Maggie. How old are you?"

"Seventeen." I hand back the bag. "Now Nick can't keep bragging that he's older than I am."

"I'll always be older than you."

"By only four months!"

He laughs. "And way more mature."

"Yeah, you're very old and wise. You're practically sprouting gray hair."

Nick finally starts the car, his mouth full of cookies. I pull out my *Guide to Northeastern Trails*, which I sometimes read during study halls. The pages call up hikes I've done with Nick—and before that, with him and Perry. The thunder of White Horse Falls, where Nick and I crept over mossy stones, closer and closer to the spray, until the mist soaked our faces and shirts. The sunset over Cannon Lake, the sky turning rose and orange and then purpling into night. The stars we saw on a December's moonlight hike with Perry, like ice crystals frozen in a blue-black sky. I breathe in, half expecting to smell that wintry air, pure and sweet with the cold, but instead I get the stale heat of a closed car in September.

I flip past these familiar hikes to the section on Eagle Mountain.

A gem of the Porte Range. Although sections of the trail require scrambling, using hands as well as feet, no mountaineering equipment (ropes, axes) is necessary. Several areas of smooth rock are exceptionally steep and should not be attempted in wet weather. Knife-edge ridges and dizzying ledges may daunt the casual hiker, but the spectacular views are well worth the climb.

Knife-edge ridges and dizzying ledges. "Have you read this hike description, Nick?"

"Yeah. Sounds good, right?"

"It's not going to rain this weekend, is it?" I snap my knife open and closed.

"Why?" Luis asks, eyeing my hands. "You gonna cut some-body if it does?"

"Yeah, she's gonna stab them with a two-inch blade," Nick snorts.

I end up at Nick's, where we often go if he doesn't play basket-ball after school. He has a photo and a topographic map of a mountain called Crystal on his bedroom wall. I study the harsh gray rock of its summit, cold and barren as the moon. Surely Eagle will be gentler than that? Crystal's in the Cinnamon Range, a couple of hours to our north, but Eagle's in the Porte range, the smaller mountains to our south.

I flop onto the bed and stare at the ceiling. I have a choice of two pictures in my mind: the "exceptionally steep" slopes of Eagle, which I can only imagine, or Raleigh Barringer's sneer. Terrific.

"Anything good up there?" Nick says, lying down beside me.

"Um," I say, wanting and not wanting to talk about Raleigh, to spill out the fear that's been locked in my chest all afternoon. Instead, I ask, "You sure you want to climb a mountain?"

"Yeah. Don't you?"

We've always craved new adventures, always driven each other. *Let's hike farther. Let's try this hike in winter. Let's do the loop* and *the spur this time.* I like the power that comes from pushing myself harder than I thought I could . . . but that doesn't mean it's easy. Nick either worries less than I do about failing, or else he hides it better.

"Oh, absolutely," I say. "I also want to whack myself on the head with a hammer."

He laughs. "You'll love it. Three or four hours of climbing straight up. You can start thinking now about how you're going to thank me."

I poke him in the stomach. He flinches but laughs again. When my hand moves in for another jab, he grabs my wrist. "Watch it," he teases. I try to spring on top of him, but he holds me off easily. In fact, he's still laughing while holding me up above him, which is downright insulting.

"I need to take karate or something," I pant.

"I'll teach you."

Our voices drop as he lowers me closer to him. Our eyes are fixed on each other, watching for sudden moves.

"You don't know karate," I say.

"That could be a problem."

Nick is one of the few people I can look in the face, but now there's a new kind of danger between us, a charge that makes me want to squirm. I want to sink the rest of the way down on top of him, and at the same time I want to push away, to leap off the bed in embarrassment. I've lost track of what we were saying. Something about . . . karate?

His phone rings. "I should get that," he says, not moving.

"Yeah, you should."

But it's another moment before he rolls me off him and leans over to grab his phone. "Yeah," he answers.

I can't hear the words on the other end, but I hear the voice, rising and falling, flooding the phone. I would know who it is even if the ringtone hadn't tipped me off—a snippet of Beethoven's Seventh, one of Nick's father's favorite pieces. "Yeah," Nick says, every minute or so. "Uh-huh. Yes."

While I wait for him to finish, my eyes roam through the room. I've seen everything in here a thousand times before: the heaps of laundry on the chair and floor. The backpack and water bottles and the rest of his hiking gear in the corner. The faded blue-and-brown quilt beneath us, with a smear of dirt from when Nick forgets to take off his boots before he lies down.

I can't help wondering what would've happened if the phone hadn't rung. If we'd kept lying face-to-face, if the gap between us had narrowed to nothing.

I've only kissed one boy before, and it was about as romantic as flossing my teeth. On Christmas Eve in eighth grade, Carl Gurney kissed me in the church parking lot while our parents were busy talking. Since Carl didn't go to my school, he didn't know how much of an outcast I was, how I'd expected to be unkissed forever.

The whole thing was over before I realized what was happening. "Merry Christmas," he gasped, before planting his rubbery lips on my mouth. A few days later, his family moved to South Africa. I thought maybe he'd kissed me *because* he was moving away—kind of a last chance, something he'd dared himself to do.

That's my entire history of success with the opposite sex. So it's hard to believe that Nick and I are on the verge of sudden passion.

"I haven't thought about that yet," Nick says into the phone. "No, Dad . . . that's not realistic."

If I'm going to lust after any guy, it should probably be Luis. He's warm and open and not too hard for me to talk to. We both like music; he moves as if he always hears it playing inside his head. He has smooth skin, full lips, an easy smile.

But he's *too* gorgeous, with a perfection that has no rough edges to grab on to. Nick is more average looking: dark hair, brown eyes. Neither ugly nor swooningly handsome. So tall that he sometimes doesn't know what to do with his knees and elbows—though that's mostly indoors. Outdoors, he's always at home. On the trails or a basketball court, he fits.

"Dad, it's not the money. . . ." Nick taps the mattress. "I mean, it's not *just* the money. . . ."

Not that I should be lusting after him, either. It could derail our whole friendship.

Looking for distraction, I reach over the side of the bed, dig through my backpack, and find my mushroom guide.

I've always found mushrooms more interesting than birds or insects or anything else we see on the trails. Maybe it's the fact that some mushrooms are edible, and others can kill you— it's that wild contrast, that sense of risk. There's also the fact that mushrooms stand still long enough to let you identify them. Unlike, say, birds.

"It has nothing to do with Mom," Nick says. "Don't—" He stops abruptly, holds the phone away from him, and stares at it. "Oh, go ahead, take that call," he says to the air. He clicks off the phone and drops it.

"That sounded like fun," I say.

"Sometimes I wonder how a guy as smart as he is can keep pretending I have an Ivy League future."

"Why do you think you don't?"

"You've met me, right?" He takes the book from my hand, his fingers brushing my skin, and flips through the pages of the guide. I've shown him its mushrooms before: some edible, some poisonous. "Are there any in here that make parents see reality?" he says.

"There should be." Unable to forget the worst part of my day—homing in on it the way you poke at a sore spot—I say, "And there should be one to send Raleigh Barringer back where she came from."

"Yeah, I heard Sylvie mention her. I've seen her around. Is she one of the ones who—"

"Yes."

Nick and I didn't go to the same junior high, but our moms are nurses at the same hospital, and he met me during the Raleigh Years. He knows I used to daydream about feeding Raleigh toadstool stew.

"I know what you could use," he says. He rests the mushroom guide on the bed, gets up, and pulls his backpack out of the corner of the room. He sets it beside the bed and opens the zippers. Its compartments gape, ready to be packed. "Just keep thinking about Saturday."

It's a sign, a promise. In spite of my doubts, I can't wait to set my feet on the trail. Our eyes lock long enough for an awkward silence to build between us, and then we both look away. A thrill rises in me, part fear and part joy, sparked by that look, and the open pack on the floor, and the knife in my pocket.

four

After a birthday dinner with my parents (my favorite roast chicken; Mom singing loudly off-key after a single glass of wine; Dad carrying in the coconut cake he picked up at the bakery), I go up to my room and call Sylvie.

"Hey, Maggie—can you tell me why cotangents are important? Will I ever need to know this again?" She sighs. "I'm drowning in homework."

"So am I, but I'm putting it off as long as possible."

"Well, I'm trying to get through this so I can go out with Wendy. I haven't seen her in a week."

Wendy is Sylvie's girlfriend. She goes to Hollander University and is about a thousand times more sophisticated than I am. She never looks sloppy, even in sweats. She already knows three languages, thanks to her family's globe-circling lifestyle, and is learning a fourth. She knows where to stay in Nairobi, how to navigate the streets and canals of Venice, what to eat in Buenos Aires, and what the exchange rate is in Mumbai. Once when Sylvie and I visited her dorm, she was lying there reading a book about the global causes of economic inequalities—and not for a class, either. Just because she wanted to.

I know I should let Sylvie go, but I linger on the phone. I want to ask about Raleigh, who is apparently now on the yearbook committee with Sylvie, but the questions pile up in my mind, unasked. How long has Raleigh been back from Italy? Has she mentioned my name, and if so, what did she say? How many allies is she gathering around her this time?

I'm scared of the answers. I need to know—it's a matter of survival— but I don't *want* to know. At the very edges of my mind, I still hear Raleigh's screech.

"Is something wrong?" Sylvie asks.

"No . . ."

"Well, I should go. Once I figure out what a cotangent is, I can go meet Wendy."

"Say hi to her for me."

When we hang up, I take out Nick's knife. Opening it, I admire the gleaming blade, beautifully sharp even if it is only two inches long. I work the miniature scissors. Then I touch the polished stone and the silver links of the necklace around my neck.

My parents gave me gifts, too, of course: sheet music and money, both of which I wanted, and clothes, which I didn't want as much, especially the ruffled shirt Mom says I can wear "someplace dressy." Since I will not be hosting state dinners or signing treaties any time soon, I doubt I'll find the right occasion for it. But the necklace and the knife are special because they're from people who aren't required by blood to give me anything. I cradle the knife in my hands, feel its weight, and touch the necklace again. Somehow it comforts me that both gifts are made of metal. They seem more permanent that way.

I go downstairs to try out the new music on the piano. I used to play every day in junior high, filling the house with waves of sound. I pounded out my anger and my fear of the school halls.

My playing has dropped off in the past couple of years, though. After I started high school, playing felt less urgent, harder to make time for. Last year when my old teacher stopped giving lessons, I didn't even look for a new one.

It takes a lot of energy to bring music to life, and then to sharpen it, to master it. Channeling a complicated piece is like taming a tiger: you set all these sounds in motion. You start themes, establish a rhythm, and then you have to keep it going. You've unleashed a tiger in the room and now you have to use every note and rest to show off its power and beauty, while keeping it under control. If you slip, a claw swipes at your leg or slashes a hole in your wall. I used to release that beast every day and control it, put it through its paces.

High school has been calmer—or I've been calmer, I'm not sure. Now the tiger mostly naps in a corner of the room. But today I'm a little hungry for that feeling again, a little restless.

I run through some old songs before trying the new pieces.

"Glad you like the music," Dad says, touching my shoulder on his way through the room.

Although Raleigh Barringer has the same lunch period as me, I manage to avoid her for days. I sit with Nick and pretend that a protective barrier surrounds our table. If it's one of the occasions when he prefers grunting and nodding to conversation, then I text Sylvie, who is usually at some club meeting. It doesn't matter whether I have much to say. Just touching base with her reassures me. It lets me know I'm no longer alone, the way I was in junior high. It reminds me the world is bigger than this cafeteria.

The salad bar has mysterious brown things on it today, I text her on Wednesday. I have no idea what they are. Nick dared me to eat one.

A minute later, I add: Nick says he will eat one of the brown things if I do. I'm thinking there should be money in this.

And then: Now Nick says I shouldn't want money. I should do it for the sake of adventure.

Sylvie replies: Nick has a strange definition of adventure.

I laugh and show that one to Nick.

"She's just finding that out?" he says.

Then Sylvie texts: You shouldn't do it because if you have a bad reaction and go to the hospital, they'll ask what you ate, and you'll say: a brown thing. And they'll say, but what was it? And you'll have to say, I don't know. And they'll say, why did you eat something when you didn't even know what it was?

I answer: You have a point. Also, I don't really want to eat a mysterious brown thing. Even for adventure.

In this way, I'm determined to keep my own little world alive, as if the rest of the cafeteria doesn't matter. Walling off Raleigh, pretending not to hear her even when she's braying ten feet from me, is something I perfected in junior high. It's strange how my stone-faced tunnel-vision abilities have come right back, though I haven't used them much since the end of eighth grade.

This is how I used to feel every day.

Raleigh had so many followers in junior high; I never knew where the attacks would come from. But our high school draws students from two junior highs and two middle schools, so the old pool of Maggie-haters has been diluted. And in high school it's not considered okay to beat up on the losers so openly. It reeks of trying too hard, of having no life of your own.

Even so—if anyone can figure out a way to carry it off, if anyone can stir an entire school against a single person, it'll be Raleigh. Which means that I can never completely relax.

On Thursday, Raleigh catches me off guard in the hall between history and English. Somewhere behind me, she squeals, "I don't belieeeve it!" I react instantly, fleeing from her voice, that piercing *eeeee*. Reaching the girls' room, I glance under the stalls for feet. I lock myself in and press my forehead against the cold metal of the door—all this before stopping to think, before asking myself what I'm doing.

I've watched Raleigh flip her shiny, black hair, gliding down the school halls with her head up. I've heard her voice plenty of times since she's been back. So I don't know why hearing it now zaps me this way, fries my nerves.

It's something about that note in her voice: the note of danger, the exact frequency of trouble. "She's heeere," Raleigh would call when I appeared at school every morning, signaling the start of the day's attacks. "Oh, Maggieee," she would sing out, and it was always the opening to an insult, a threat, or an order. "Oh, Maggieee, *cover* yourself, so your ugly face won't make me throw up!"

I have to stop these flashbacks.

I belong here just as much as she does. I can't crawl through the halls on my belly until we graduate. I only hope she didn't see me running, that she didn't catch the scent of my fear the way a shark smells blood in the ocean.

Slippery-palmed, dry-tongued, I force myself to open the door.

'm in no mood to dissect a frog with Adriana Lippold this afternoon, but that is what I'm destined to do. Formaldehyde prickles the inside of my nose as we snip and slice silently, identifying the organs and drawing them on our lab diagrams. I've never thought of Adriana as particularly smart—maybe because of her obsession with makeup and clothes, or the way she always trotted around at Raleigh's heels—but I realize now there's no reason to assume she's stupid. In fact, maybe the surgical precision she once used to dismantle my ego should've prepared me for her skill at cutting up dead animals.

"Wow, look how big the liver is," she says.

"Yeah." I've been thinking the same thing. At first, I thought the liver was the stomach, but the stomach is much smaller than I'd expected.

We exchange a few more remarks about frog anatomy. At one point I study her face, wondering what's going on behind the frosting of blush and mascara and lip gloss. I wish I knew why she used to get such joy from helping Raleigh tear me apart, how she could've liked the taste of that poison in her mouth.

And I can't help wondering if she and Raleigh are already plotting against me, starting up a new wave of anti-Maggie operations. Maybe they've just been waiting for Raleigh to get over her jet lag and gather her army of haters.

When Adriana looks up at me, I turn back to the frog, steadying my hands on the pins and scalpel. *Concentrate,* I tell myself. *This is your job.*

Maggie Camden, Amphibian Coroner. Sounds like a TV show nobody would ever watch. But I get through the rest of the lab.

Friday night marks my survival of another week of school. I sleep over at Nick's so we can get an early start for Eagle Mountain the next morning. Phoebe, Nick's mom, is in bed when I get there, but Perry is watching a martial-arts movie and flipping through atlases.

Perry loves maps—not antique maps, but maps from fifty or sixty years ago, including road maps. He buys tons of them at yard sales. He frames his favorites and hangs them on the walls, even though Phoebe isn't crazy about them. "Not another one, Perry," she'll groan. But I'm so used to them that an aerial view of Yellowstone Park will forever remind me of their living room, and an old road map of Nevada means we're in the upstairs hall. Perry gave Nick the topographic map of Crystal Mountain that hangs on his bedroom wall next to the photograph of its summit.

"Eagle's a good hike. I envy you," Perry tells us now, taking his booted feet off the coffee table. One thing I love about Nick's house is that you can put your feet up on the furniture whenever you want. Unlike at my house, where wood finish is practically sacred. This is one of Dad's few annoying quirks—because he loves working with wood, he can't bear to see it treated casually. We spend half our lives hunting down coasters to put under our drinks.

"Yeah, I can't wait to get up there," Nick says.

"Me neither." I want to get out into the woods, to wash the staleness of school halls out of my lungs, to take a full breath without worrying about Raleigh around the next corner.

Perry clicks off his movie. "One thing, Nick. Your dad called. He said he couldn't get through on your phone."

"What did he want?"

"He didn't say. Just that he'll try to reach you again." Perry appears to be on the verge of saying more. This happens a lot when he talks about Nick's dad. Like he has to stop himself from whatever he really wants to say. In the four years he's been married to Phoebe, I've never heard him say anything bad about Nick's father, but he does seem to swallow a lot of words unsaid.

Nick gives a sour laugh. "Must've been real important."

Nick and I hang out in the living room for a while, going over the description of Eagle and planning what to bring for lunch. We bend over the trail map, our knees and arms brushing, our faces barely an inch apart. I'm hyperaware of the mixed soap-and-sweat scent of his skin, of my hair brushing his cheek, of his leg against mine. I follow his finger along a mountain ridge with my eyes, wondering what would happen if I acted on this heat. It's hard for me to imagine it working smoothly, the two of us sliding into each other's arms like some movie couple. The way we're sitting, we'd probably bump elbows, get tangled up in the map. And then there are our legs: What would we do with them?

For all I know, kissing Nick might be just as disappointing as kissing Carl Gurney. I'm not sure how much experience Nick has. Over the summer, he went out once or twice with a girl from the garden center where he worked. And last year, Luis teased him about some girl he met at a party thrown by one of the basketball players. But he's never had a real girlfriend, never spent much time with any girl but me.

Does that mean there's potential? Or does it mean I'll always be just a friend, part of the scenery, no more lust-worthy than one of the thousands of trees we've hiked past?

I shouldn't even be using up brain cells on this, since the mountain will give me enough to worry about. The contour lines on the map are closely drawn, dense, signaling steepness.

It'll be a long hard haul upward, tougher than anything we've hiked before. Phrases from the guidebook haunt me: *knife-edge ridges, dizzying ledges.*

Before I go to bed on the foldout couch beneath the Yellowstone map, I slip out to the hall and study the photo of Perry on top of Eagle Mountain. He was slimmer then, with more hair and a blissful grin. The camera is focused on him, and I can't see much of the view. It's mostly sky. I'm trying to get a sense of how high Eagle is—well, I know that, I know its surveyed measurement, but I'm trying to get a sense of how high it *feels*.

I want to stand up there. Whenever Nick and I finish a day of hiking, especially when we do something I wasn't sure I was capable of, I get a surge of power. It's like the feeling of mastering a piece on the piano, but it's a feeling of physical strength, too. Sometimes I think that if I'd started hiking before junior high, Raleigh wouldn't have been able to push me around the way she did. I would've been too strong.

The thought of summiting Eagle thrills me as much as it scares me. I felt the pull of the Porte Range all the way from Silver Creek, when it was just a series of peaks on a distant horizon. It'll be harder than anything we've ever done, so the power will be greater. And with Raleigh back in town, I need that power.

But whatever answers I'm looking for, they're not in this

photo. I return to the living room and line up all my hiking gear: boots, water bottles, rain suit, knife, flashlight, first-aid kit, trail guide, mushroom guide. My boots smell of leather. They've been rubbed satiny from previous hikes, but when I brush them with my fingertips, chocolate-colored dirt dusts my skin.

I stow most of the items in my pack, leaving the bottles out to fill in the morning. Then I sit staring at my gear. It's so much more organized than my brain, where more problems than I can tackle at once are wheeling and fighting for space: the challenge of the mountain, the threat of Raleigh, the strange new undercurrent between Nick and me. All of it will come to Eagle Mountain with us, carried in the pit of my stomach.

six

I dream of Raleigh Barringer. She's on the mountain with us. While jeering at me, she twists her ankle. She needs us to help her down. While she sits on the ground, crying and clutching her ankle, I say, in the exact tone of voice she used on me in junior high: "Oh, shut up. Don't be such a baby." I tower over her; she shrinks beneath my eyes.

I wake up sweating. It's not quite six o'clock.

I sit for a minute watching the ghostly blue light of the pre-dawn sky, listening to the whirring of the last crickets of the season, letting the dream—with its strange mix of fear and power—melt away. Fat chance I'd ever have the upper hand over Raleigh.

I love this time of day, when nobody else is around, when everything is clean and fresh, when there's more space to breathe. Once I've filled my lungs with the morning, I tiptoe upstairs, careful not to wake Nick's mom and stepdad. Naturally, Nick's door is still shut.

I tap lightly and push open the door to his room. He's a blanket-covered bundle, slug-like. I plop down on the end of the bed, drawing an "oof" from him.

"Ready for Eagle?" I say.

"Mm."

"You don't sound ready."

"Jesus, Maggie." His voice rasps and rumbles, like a car with a bad starter. I smile to myself at that thought: *Nick has a bad starter.* That must be why he has such trouble getting up in the morning.

"This is your wake-up call." I jounce the bed, and he rolls over.

"More like my wake-up pain in the ass." Yawning, he frees his head from the sheets and glares at me. He's always had the sort of pale-skinned, dark-haired complexion that's gorgeous when he's had enough sleep, and ghoulish when he hasn't. And right now he has that pasty, grimy, up-all-night look. "Why don't you go down and start some coffee?"

"Fine. But I'm coming back up here in five minutes and if I find you snoring—"

"*OUT.*"

I figure he's awake enough now to stay that way. I slip out of his room.

*   *   *

Nick loves his coffee scorching and bitter. I'd sooner drink drain cleaner myself, but I'm willing to brew a pot if it will get him moving. I pad around the quiet kitchen in my socks. As I slide the filter full of rich, dark grounds into the machine, the door that leads out to the driveway opens.

Nick's father, Dr. Cleary, stands there holding the screen door. "Good morning, Margaret. Mind if I come in?"

"Oh—good morning. Yes, come in."

I always feel stupid around Dr. Cleary, as if I'm supposed to use bigger words and more formal sentences than I normally do. He's a scientific researcher with a dozen initials after his name, and he's been doing something in his lab with protein folding that makes the other scientists salivate and murmur words like *Nobel*. I don't know exactly what is so thrilling about protein folding, which is probably one reason I feel stupid. Not that I know all the details of my own parents' jobs, but my dad monitors the electrical grid for Mid-Regional Power, and my mom is a nurse, so at least I understand the main point of what they do.

"You're here early. Did you stay overnight again?" Dr. Cleary says. "Has my son dragged his body out of bed yet?" He sits at the kitchen table. His shirt is wrinkled, but his sleek, black hair is freshly combed, and he's wearing a tie. Stubble peppers his cheeks and chin, and his face has the same skim-milk tint that Nick's gets after too little sleep.

"Nick and I are going hiking." I fiddle with the coffeemaker, double-checking the settings even though I know they're correct.

"Ah. Right. Hiking." His voice has a weary undertone. I think he's been hoping Nick will outgrow his love of hiking. As if it's cute for us to "play" in the woods, but someday we'll do something more worthwhile.

Nick stumbles into the room. He homes in on the coffee-maker—and then stops in mid-step, mid-yawn.

"What are you doing here so early?" he asks his father.

Dr. Cleary laughs. "I never went to bed."

"Oh."

Nick has told me his dad pulls all-nighters sometimes, especially if he has an important grant proposal to write, or new data coming in from a late-running experiment.

A stream of coffee hisses into the glass pot. We all stare at it.

My backbone itches. I strain for anything I could possibly say to Nick's father. I can't ask about his work because I don't understand it. I doubt he'd be interested in the daily inner workings of West Valley High School ("Guess what, Dr. Cleary! We now have blue trays in the cafeteria, in addition to the old brown ones!"). And Nick is no help, standing there with a glazed look on his face that suggests he's technically still asleep. "Coffee?" I ask, just to say something. I grip the handle of the pot, though liquid is still spurting down into it.

"Hold on there, Margaret," Nick's father says. "It isn't ready yet."

"Oh, I guess you're right."

I sit at the kitchen table, across from Dr. Cleary. I trace the grain in the fake-wood tabletop while Nick hovers over the coffeemaker. I half expect Nick to stick his mouth right under the spout and catch the coffee as it squirts out.

"How's school?" Nick's father asks him.

"Fine."

"I hear you're having trouble in history."

Nick shrugs.

"Do you study enough? How much do you study?"

Nick sits down at the table with a cup of coffee. I don't expect him to give me one because he knows I hate it, but he doesn't offer his father any, either. After a minute, Dr. Cleary gets up and pours it himself.

"I'm going to see your grandmother and your uncle today," he says. "I thought you could come along."

"You should've called," Nick says. "I already have plans."

"Hiking. So I understand," Dr. Cleary says dryly. He glances at me. "I'm sure Margaret won't mind if you see your family instead."

"It's not your weekend with me."

Dr. Cleary's lips tighten. "Now, that sounds like your mother talking."

Nick takes a long, slow sip. Then he sets down the coffee. "Don't bring her into this."

"Or maybe you'd be better off staying home and studying history."

Nick's face reddens, but he doesn't answer.

"Have you thought about our talk the other day?"

"No." Nick focuses on his cup like it's about to give him all the answers to the SATs.

"You can't put it off forever. Use that brain of yours."

Dr. Cleary leans over and taps the side of Nick's head, his forefinger giving two slow, deliberate thumps against Nick's scalp. Nick doesn't even blink.

After a minute, Dr. Cleary drains his mug and sets it in the middle of the table. We all look at it like it's a precious work of art he has presented for our consideration.

"Thank you for the coffee," he says, and stalks out of the house.

Nick and I are still sitting at the table when Perry comes downstairs, his boots thudding heavily against the floor. Perry works construction, but even when he isn't working, he wears boots. I've never seen anything else on his feet.

"Six o'clock on a weekday, I couldn't get you out of bed if the house was on fire," Perry says. "Six o'clock on a Saturday, and here you are." He grins, setting a skillet on one burner. "You kids want some eggs?"

"No, thanks," Nick says. "We'll eat on the road." We always have a big breakfast at a diner on Route 27 when we hike; it's part of our ritual. I suspect that some secret part of our brains even believes we won't be able to climb the mountain if we don't have a Bird's Nest Diner breakfast.

Phoebe trudges into the room, her eyes open only wide enough to keep her from banging into the table. She zeroes in on the coffee. Nick pours her a cup. As soon as she has pried her eyes open halfway, she says, "Maggie, good morning. I hear you're climbing Eagle today."

"Assuming I can make it."

"We'll make it," Nick says.

"I wish I were going with you." Perry cracks his knuckles while he waits for the skillet to heat.

"You could," I say.

"If these old knees would let me. You kids have fun—and don't forget to check in at the trailhead."

"Yes," Phoebe adds. "And call me when you get off the trail so I know you're okay."

"We'll be fine," Nick says. "It's not Everest."

I make a face at him behind his mother's back, since I know that Everest comment is aimed at me, too. He grins.

"Call anyway," Phoebe says.

"If it makes you feel better." Nick, who has towered over her since he was a freshman, drops a kiss on top of her head. I notice he hasn't mentioned his father's visit. Maybe it's because any mention of Dr. Cleary tends to bring out a dent of worry in Phoebe's forehead, right between her eyes.

Nick and I pause in the living room to watch the weather on TV. While we wait for the forecast, I sneak a glance at him. The TV paints a white glow along the edge of Nick's nose, cheek, and chin. His eyes don't move from the screen, which is showing a razor-blade commercial about the "closest shave ever." I can't stop hearing those two thumps of his father's finger against his skull: more than a tap, less than a hit, and profoundly weird. I will never understand Nick's father.

I reach toward Nick while we're both still facing the TV. My fingertips bump the back of his hand. He doesn't give any indication of feeling that. I rest my fingers against his, wanting at least to bring him out of his father-induced moodiness, maybe wanting more. But when he turns his head toward me, I pull back my hand.

Before we can say anything, the forecast comes on: mostly cloudy, 30 percent chance of showers. I think of the line in the guidebook about how Eagle can be dangerous in the rain, but 30 percent doesn't seem big enough to cancel our trip. I've psyched myself up for today. If we change the timing, it might make it harder the next time.

I don't need it to be harder.

We step out into the chill of the morning. The heaviness of my pack always surprises me when I first heave the strap over my shoulder. Nick clears his throat and gives a rough morning cough.

My feet brush dew from the grass. Every surface inside the car is morning-cold. We pack our gear in the back. I'm careful not to touch Nick again. When he starts the car, the freedom of the day in front of us rises, and it almost feels as if we can fly.

Eagle waits for us.

seven

W e squabble in the diner over whether grape jam is better than strawberry (the latest episode in our fiery, years-long Great Jam Debate). I pretend that the sight of Nick putting salsa on scrambled eggs doesn't give me indigestion.

When I ask him if I can have the peeled orange wedge that decorates his plate, he picks it up and brings it right to my mouth. My lips brush his fingers, even though I'm trying not to touch him. He absently sucks the orange juice from his hand while he looks over the check. Is he as aware of these things as I am, of this new tension between us? Or to him, is it all as casual as the other ways we've touched in the past: brushing dirt off each other's backs, inspecting for ticks, holding hands to steady ourselves while on stepping-stones?

As Nick and I start up the Eagle Mountain trail, we fall into our usual rhythm. The first three steps feel wonderful; I could eat up the world in half a dozen strides. And then the weight of the pack descends on my shoulders and hips, and my boots gain ten pounds apiece. I stumble over a rock.

I settle one layer deeper into the hike, and the world settles around me. Now I'm not worrying about running into Raleigh Barringer in the school hall. I'm not analyzing Nick's every move in my direction. I'm not counting the minutes until the school bell rings or ticking off a list of math problems to solve. I'm here, and this is where I want to be.

Here, with the ferns and moss, with the scabbed bark of trees, the dank smell of mud, the sweet aroma of dead leaves.

Here, with the stream bubbling alongside us, soothing, gabbling in a language that I both understand and don't understand.

Here, with a rattlesnake that I almost step on.

"Whoa," Nick says as we freeze.

The snake coils in the middle of the path, shaking its tail in the air. We can't hear the rattle over the rush of the creek beside us, but we can certainly see it. We back up a few steps, hoping it will uncoil and glide away, like every other snake we've ever met.

No such luck. This one holds its ground. I've never had a snake rattle at me before, and even though it's a few feet away, my teeth clench.

"Maybe we can go around it," Nick says.

"You mean jump off the cliff on the right, or climb up the cliff on the left?"

"Those aren't cliffs."

All right, they aren't *exactly* cliffs. But the ground on the right of the trail drops down a stony incline to a white-water creek, and on the left rises a rocky slope studded with stubby trees and bushes.

"I bet the trail's wide enough for us to squeeze by," Nick says.

"Are you crazy?"

"How much striking distance do they have anyway—like, half a body length, right?"

I don't remember, and I don't want to test it out. Besides, since the snake is coiled, it's hard to tell how long it is. "Right, Nick. You ask the snake to lie straight along the ground, and I'll get out the yardstick I happened to bring, and we'll measure it."

"Okay, okay." He sits on a rock at the side of the trail and pulls out his water bottle. I choose another rock. The snake stops rattling but stays where it is, a spiral in the middle of the trail.

I mentally rehearse everything I've learned in first aid about treating snakebites. Then, to distract myself, I get out my guidebook to fungi and look up a crimson-topped mushroom growing near us. "*Russula*," I tell Nick. "'The sickener.' It's poisonous."

"Are you suggesting we feed it to the snake?"

"Uh, yeah, I'm sure he'll open wide for us."

I love that name, "the sickener." It leaves no doubt what the mushroom does. What I find especially interesting are the entries for some of the other mushrooms that say, "Edibility unknown." It's hard to believe there are mushrooms nobody has ever tried yet.

Not that I'm planning to be the first.

"That snake's not going anywhere," Nick says. "Maybe I can get a long stick and move it."

"No way."

"Most times when they bite people, they don't even inject venom."

"Oh, brilliant, Nick. That's very comforting. I can't believe I thought about—" I choke myself off just in time. I've almost said *I can't believe I thought about kissing you.* I'm so used to joking with Nick about whatever pops into my head that I don't know when to shut up.

"Thought about what?" But he's looking around for a stick and doesn't notice that I don't answer him.

I can see I need to take action here before we both end up stretched out lifeless on the ground, puncture marks in our legs. "All right, let's try going around him. Up the cliff."

"It's not a cliff," Nick says again. As if calling it something else will make the climb easier.

We scramble upward, using our hands as well as our feet. The rock scratches our fingers and blunts our nails. It's impossible to keep my fingers and toes away from every cranny that could harbor one of our snake friend's relatives, so I plow ahead, straining my ears for any hint of a rattle. Grit wedges itself under my nails. Step-by-step, we angle back toward the trail. The snake still rests in the middle of the path behind us, and that is where Nick and I leave it.

"Do you think that snake was a sign?" I ask Nick.

"A sign of what?"

"That we shouldn't climb this mountain." In fact, it hasn't been a day of good omens at all, first with Nick's father and now the snake.

"You know what it's a sign of, Maggie?"

"What?"

"That snakes live around here."

In junior high, when I was desperate for any measure of control, I searched for omens everywhere. If the first crocus of February opened, if the cafeteria had my favorite enchiladas for lunch, or if we got to run a mile in gym class instead of having to play team sports, it was good. Cold rain, the piano getting out of tune, and a hole in my favorite shoes were all bad signs.

I stopped hunting for omens when I realized that none of them ever predicted how harsh Raleigh and company would be on any given day. A good day was when they ignored me. A bad day was when they came after me. But it was dictated by nothing I could see or control. Nothing I wore, said, ate, or did seemed to have the slightest effect. Only Raleigh's whim.

But every now and then, I still catch myself doing it, trying to predict good or bad luck.

Clouds shroud the sun. The air on Eagle Mountain is heavy, moist, with a tinge of mildew. Mosquito clouds hover in a couple of soggy spots along the trail. We spot some red and golden leaves, but most of the forest is still green.

"Ever wish you could live out here?" Nick says.

"Sometimes." This was especially true in junior high, when I wanted to drop out of school and move into the forest. I imagined living on fish, squirrels, berries, and mushrooms. And even though I've always known on some level that it wouldn't work (Who do I think I am—Davy Crockett? How would I catch and skin a squirrel? What if I needed antibiotics or an appendectomy?), I still daydream about getting away. "How about you?"

"Yeah, all the time. You know, we could do it. Fish and hunt and harvest wild plants. Sleep on pine needles, and only get up when we feel like it."

Trust Nick to name the lack of an alarm clock as a chief perk. But I can't deny it's a great daydream. If we were slightly crazier, we could probably talk each other into it. For a few days, at least.

But the reality is, it rains and snows out here. And there

are certain things I'd rather not live without, like hot showers. "You'd miss basketball, though," I say. "And coffee."

"True." He grins. "Guess I'll stay in civilization after all."

As Nick and I climb upward, the sky darkens and the air thickens. Everything smells of mushrooms now, the forest getting damper and cooler by the minute. The cloud ceiling presses down on us.

"You bring your rain gear?" Nick asks.

"Of course." Perry drilled that into us. Nick and I would no more forget our rain gear than we would forget our hands and feet. But I keep remembering that line in the guidebook: *Several areas of smooth rock are exceptionally steep and should not be attempted in wet weather.* I picture us skidding down a wet rock slope, bones cracking along the way. We've hiked through rain before, but that was on flat ground with plenty of traction. Rain must turn the slanted, featureless rock of Eagle's higher slopes into a water slide.

We sniff the air, gauging the closeness of the storm. This is the decision point, our last chance to turn back. If we go up this next section, it will be better to keep on and go over the top, descending the White Arrow trail, rather than come back down this side.

"What do you think?" I ask Nick as we inspect the pieces of blank white sky between tree branches.

"I say we go up. There's no thunder, and it's not raining yet."
He scratches his jaw. "But it's up to you."

Sweat collects under my shirt, slimy on my skin. I cup my
hands, as if I can feel the weight of our choices: *Go on. Turn
around.*

It's hard to break this upward momentum, hard not to feel
like a failure for doing it. When I think about descending now,
the part of my mind that still speaks in Raleigh Barringer's
voice says, *Why leave so early, Maggie? Can't handle it?* I hate the
vision of myself that her voice conjures up: weak and cringing
and awkward, as if I deserve everything she ever said.

But it's more than that. I think of Perry's blissful grin in his
summit picture, and I want to know what that feels like. I want
to reach the top.

I catch Nick's eye. He says nothing, only waits for my decision. "Yes, let's keep going," I say, and he smiles.

Here the mountain gets steeper, the rocks bigger. We're using
our hands most of the time now, scaling boulders. Sometimes
we hit stretches of bare stone, and we inch upward, finding the
ripples and cracks and knobs that form footholds. In a couple
of places, where the slant is near vertical, wooden ladders have
been bolted into the rock.

The trees around us get shorter as we near the bald top of
the mountain. A breeze lifts the hair away from my neck and

hisses in my ear. A wet drop splats against my cheek. When five minutes go by without another, I start to relax.

And then the second drop hits me.

"It's raining," I tell Nick.

"I know."

We stop to pull on our rain suits. The fabric is supposed to breathe, but with my skin already sweaty and the air turning liquid, there's no escaping the moisture. I make sure the pit zips and the front zipper are open, and continue to claw my way up the cold, wet rock. It's different from the flat-ground hiking we've done before, because there's this whole new dimension to deal with: the vertical. Often the span of a step seems impossible, a gap my legs can't possibly cover, but I reach and I stretch and I cover it somehow. Other times, I'll stop at a rock outcropping, clueless about how to scale it, but I learn to pick out the dimples and shelves I can use to help myself up.

Nick's above me, his long arms and legs pulling him upward faster than I can go, but he waits for me at every convenient ledge. We're both panting, our skin shiny. Our stomachs rumble, but we don't stop for lunch, though it's after twelve.

I try not to look out over the valley too much. As long as I focus on the rock beneath my feet, the tree branches jutting over the trail, I'm okay. But when I glance at the drop-off, the view whirls and the sky wheels around me; the mountain seems to fall away from beneath my feet. I fix my eyes on solid rock again, and the world clicks back into place.

When we break out above tree line, the full force of the rain slashes into us. We retreat into the trees again. Huddling below the signs that say: ALPINE ZONE—WATCH WHERE YOU STEP and ELEVATION 4,000 FEET—NO CAMPING BEYOND THIS POINT, we gasp to catch the breath that the storm has stolen from us.

"Wow," I say.

Nick wipes rain off his face.

"This might not be the best idea we've ever had," I say.

"You think?" he says, and then we're both laughing, the laughter a relief valve for the nervousness just underneath.

As we move back onto the trail, the rain blasts us, soaking into every crevice: the opening around my face, the narrow gap around my cuffs, the zippers I opened to let in cool air.

The top of Eagle Mountain keeps receding. I think each bump in the terrain is going to be the last one, only to top it and find another one higher.

But in spite of the pounding rain and the ache in my legs, we're making progress. My own strength is getting me up this mountain. I scale boulder after boulder, joy welling up inside me.

Nick points out a circular metal survey marker under our feet, and suddenly I realize we've reached the top.

There would probably be a view on a sunnier day. Now I see vague humps of fog-blurred hills and trees below us, but mostly it's like being inside a cloud. I'm as wet as I can get, with my jacket and pants plastered to my skin, and water dribbling down my face.

Nick wraps his arms around me, and I hug him back. "Welcome to Eagle," he says.

"Beautiful weather we're having." And for a minute we savor the summit, the giddiness of having nowhere higher to go.

"You're soaked," he says in my ear.

"So are you."

He rubs his wet cheek against mine, laughing softly. At that moment, while we cling to each other, I don't mind the rain. It dissolves the boundary between my body and the world, the boundary between Nick and me.

eight

We find the White Arrow trail on the other side of the mountain and start our descent, clambering over slippery wet boulders. In the steepest places, I sit and scoot down crab-like with my butt, hands, and feet all touching the rock. I couldn't care less if the Sitting Crab isn't a graceful position—I'm not about to break my neck.

I skid once on a wet leaf, and my stomach leaps onto my tongue, but I grip the jutting edge of a boulder to stop myself from hurtling down the trail. As much as I just want to get home where I can dry off, I force myself to go slowly, to concentrate on each step. Perry has told us that most mountain-climbing accidents occur on the way down, and I believe it.

"Think it'll rain today, Maggie?" Nick asks.

We go to Nick's place, but nobody is home to celebrate our victory. We peel off our outer gear in his kitchen, leaving it in a soggy lump next to the door, and climb rather squishily up to his room. I face the picture and the map of Crystal, thinking: *I bet I could climb you, too.*

"I should've brought another change of clothes," I say, pulling my shirt away from my skin. I've changed into dry socks and shoes—I always have extra socks when I hike—but I might as well have gone swimming in the rest of my clothes, which didn't dry much in the two hours in the car. The clothes I wore yesterday are dry but dirty.

"You want one of my T-shirts?" Nick tosses me a gargantuan piece of fabric I could use as a tent.

"Thanks. I have never been this soaked in my life."

"Me neither." He laughs and tugs at the bottom of my shirt, pretending to wring water from it. I bump against him and squeeze the bottom of his shirt the same way. We're both still full of the mountain. I try to step away, but he's holding on to my shirt.

"Nick, you should let me change."

"No, I like you the way you are."

"Very funny." I try to toss my head, and my hair moves as one wet mass. "I'm probably carrying a gallon of water in my hair alone."

He twines his hand in my hair. "That's a good survival strategy—carry extra water up here so you won't dehydrate."

"Yeah, this brain of mine is always working."

Usually, the only person who touches my hair is the girl down at The Mane Event, who always asks, "When's the last time you had this cut?" in a tone implying I've dragged my head through a swamp before presenting it to her.

But Nick does not ask me when I last cut my hair, or whether I want a shampoo, or if I want a conditioner treatment to save my raggedy ends. His hand stays in my hair, the fingers moving as if to massage my scalp.

We're breathless from laughing, but there's something else in the way we're staring at each other now, something electric and scary and delicious. His eyes search my face; his throat moves as he swallows.

He bends forward, and his mouth touches mine. He pauses, waiting for something—my reaction?—but I don't know what to do now that this is actually happening. Finally, I engage the gears in my brain, almost hearing them grind. I tilt my face up toward his and kiss him back.

He's not like Carl.

For one thing, Nick kisses slowly enough for me to feel it. And he opens his mouth. I concentrate on the point where our tongues touch. Heat spreads through me, and though his mouth feels a little strange, wetter and softer than I would have guessed, I don't want him to stop. He strokes my hair, my shoulder. He kisses my neck and I arch my back, startled by his tongue against my skin.

His mouth finds mine again. I shiver because I'm not used to being this close to anyone, especially not for this long, but I don't break away.

This is what I've wanted. Yet some small part of my brain

hangs back, asking: *What happens next? What does this mean?* My thoughts fragment, sliding and crashing into one another, their jagged edges catching. Still I keep kissing him, one hand holding on to the dry shirt he gave me, the other gripping the damp shirt he's wearing.

"Nick! Are you home?" his mom calls from the stairway, and her voice jolts Nick and me apart. Now that his tongue is no longer in my mouth, I have no idea what to say, where to pick up.

"Maggie, I—" His voice is hoarse.

"Um, I should go," I say, my blood running hot and cold, heart jumping up against the roof of my mouth as if I've had way too much caffeine. I need to think. I need to breathe. I need—

I'm out of the room, jogging down the stairs with a quick "Hi!" to Phoebe. I escape into the gray September afternoon.

It has stopped raining, which is a good thing because I have a two-mile walk home. Also I realize, several blocks from Nick's house, that I am still holding the shirt he gave me, but I have left behind my overnight bag, boots, backpack, and rain suit.

I pass through the center of town, the strip with the drugstore and the real-estate office, the gas station and the funeral home. There's also a rectangular park with a war memorial and a bronze statue of the town founder holding his fist to his chest, a gesture that is supposed to suggest his intense love for the town, but always makes me think he's having a heart attack.

I head west, trying to digest what just happened with Nick, but all I'm able to do is knead his T-shirt. I replay the kiss endlessly: his hands in my hair, his mouth sweet from the trail mix we ate in the car, his tongue on my neck.

At last I reach my own street, a row of 1950s flat-roofed boxes. I've often wondered if it was the fear of annihilation by hydrogen bomb that led the builders of my neighborhood to create all these concrete-walled bunkers, with windows so deeply recessed that our living room stays dark even in the middle of a blazing summer day. And on cloudy days, like today, it might as well be the inside of a closet.

I'm glad for the darkness, though, glad that both my parents are out. I curl up on the couch and press my cheek against the rough weave of brown-rust-gold plaid. This is the couch I come to when I'm sick. This is where I used to lie every night in junior high, worrying about the next day's tortures, trying to gather myself. Counting down to weekends, to vacations, to the end of the school year.

Now I take refuge on the couch again. Only this time, I'm not miserable. This time, I'm thinking, *So this is what it feels like to get what you want.*

Mom and I eat dinner alone, since Dad's working late at the power company. The storm must've caused outages somewhere; bad weather usually earns him overtime. When I was little, and he talked about the endless demands of "the grid," I pictured it as a huge beast—like a lion, incredibly powerful and always hungry.

We microwave a couple of trays of food and eat in the living room. PBS has a special on, featuring famous moments from all the old movies Mom loves.

During the pledge-drive break, she mutes the TV. "I need your college list, Maggie," she reminds me.

We've been talking about this list a lot lately. Mom wants us to visit schools this year, so I'll be ready to apply early in my senior year. She's been planning my college education since I popped out of the womb. Not that I mind, on one level. Whenever I go with Sylvie to visit Wendy at the university, I revel in the library, the giant bookstore, the wide yards where people sit reading or arguing about things like the Heisenberg Uncertainty Principle. And though there are plenty of beer cans strewn around, college seems like a place where it's okay to admit you have a brain.

I've already decided that I want to live away from home, and that I want someplace strong in math and science, but where I can also take music as an elective. Maybe a big school, where one small clique can't rule the campus.

But that's as far as I've gotten. Wanting to go to college isn't the same as filtering the flood of information, figuring it all out, reading about the majors and degrees and activities and requirements, making the choices. If I could snap my fingers and be transported to the right school, it would be one thing, but what if I choose wrong? What if I pick the wrong major and realize I hate what I'm studying, or discover that the professors are boring and out of touch, or learn that there are no jobs in the field? What if I end up at a place ruled by people like Raleigh and Adriana? What if the school is too big and I just feel lost?

Not that I can explain this to my mother, who never has trouble with any new situation herself—such as the block's yard sale, for which she became the committee chair after one meeting. Or the church volunteer program, which led to her being named "Helping Hand of the Year," complete with wall-dominating plaque of appreciation.

"I'm working on it," I tell her.

"Don't put it off too long. We want to get our schedule set up." The show comes back on, and Mom punches up the volume.

The next segment they're showing is Great Movie Kisses.

Actors and actresses hurl themselves at one another: clinging arms, open mouths. Bare pecs, bulging biceps, delicate female throats and shoulders. Men bend over their partners; the women arch backward. A couple rolls in the ocean surf. We're subjected to one lip-lock after another, every one of them throwing me back to that moment when Nick's mouth met mine. I feel that kiss again, taste it.

Fortunately, Mom is looking at the screen, not at me, or she might ask why all the blood is migrating to my face.

As soon as the TV couples stop making out, I jump up. "Guess I'll go upstairs."

"Already? It's early."

"Yeah, I'll read for a while."

Safe in my room, I check my messages, sure there will be something from Nick. I can't wait to read it.

But there are none.

In junior high, Raleigh and Adriana used to tell me, "No boys will ever go out with you. Nobody could ever like you." Always laughing, shrieking. Whenever I hear girls laugh high and loud like that, it still makes me shudder.

And it's their voices I hear now, looking at my empty message box, as the hopeful excitement I've carried all afternoon starts to sour.

What if he doesn't—that is, if he isn't—

He might be cringing with regret right now. Worrying that I'll see today as the start of something when it was a momentary impulse, nothing to take seriously. High from the success of climbing the mountain, carried away for a minute . . . we were jostling and bumping each other and he thought *What if* and then he went with it, but that doesn't mean he wanted anything more. . . .

I've heard girls talk in the restroom, the locker room, the cafeteria. "I thought we had a great time, and then he never called again." "I thought he liked me, but he only wanted to talk about Cindy." "He said he would text me, but he didn't." "We spent the *whole party* making out, and then he goes, 'Oh, it was just one of those things.'" "He said he didn't know I would take it so seriously." "He said it was no big deal." "He didn't answer my messages." "I never heard from him." "It ruined our whole friendship. Now he doesn't even talk to me."

This is what I was afraid of; this is what I should've remembered. This is what I didn't want to risk.

But it isn't as if Nick and I just met or randomly hooked up at a party. We've known each other for years. We've spent hours together on the trails.

He has waited without complaint for me to identify trailside mushrooms. He's listened to me ramble about gills and boletes and spores. When we share trail mix, he eats all the raisins because I won't touch them—he must've eaten thousands of extra raisins on my account. He gave me the knife I wanted. He climbed a mountain with me.

And in his room this afternoon, I didn't pin him to the wall. He didn't trip and accidentally plant his lips on my face. He knew what he was doing—and seemed to like it. As much as I could tell, having almost zero experience with guys.

So maybe something new really is starting between us.

(His tongue against my skin, his tongue in my mouth.)

But then—why the silence now?

I reach for my mushroom guide, which is usually a good distraction. But the guide is in my backpack—still at Nick's house.

No matter what I do tonight, my thoughts come back to Nick. I check my phone again. No messages.

There's no reason I have to wait for him. I could make the call myself. But what would I say?

I could pretend nothing happened. "Kiss? What kiss? Now that you mention it, I *thought* I felt something on my lips."

I could ask him what's going on. "When you kissed me, did you mean it, or was it a friends-with-benefits type of thing?"

Or I could let anxiety take over. "Why haven't you called me? You don't think I'm too needy or anything, do you?"

I could pretend I only called to get my stuff back. "I thought if you weren't busy, I could come pick up the things I forgot to take with me . . . not that there's any special *reason* I was distracted when I left your house. . . ."

Then again, I could simply be honest: "Did you like it as much as I did?"

I'm starting to realize what's at stake. If Nick and I veer down the wrong path now, we could wreck everything. We could end up not even being friends.

No more hiking. No more talking or texting with him. A break with Nick would leave me alone on the school bus, isolated at lunch. No more sitting around his kitchen or watching movies in his living room on rainy Sunday afternoons with our feet up on the coffee table. Worst of all would be losing the one person who loves being out in the woods as much as I do, loves the smell of damp bark and pine sap, the softness of moss and the crunch of fall leaves, the solid feel of rocks and dirt underfoot.

I carry my phone downstairs and sit at the piano bench, where I pound out "Nightwaves"—a piece my old piano teacher composed for me. He said he wrote it to showcase my fondness for the keys below middle C: the deeper, darker, stormier notes.

The "Nightwaves" roll over me. But I'm also keeping an ear open for the beep of my phone. Just in case Nick figures out this thing before I do, and calls to help me make sense of it.

nine

Sunday is hot and steamy, a throwback to midsummer. I ride my bike over to Sylvie's, where she is making tray after tray of brownies for a bake sale to support the school activities fund. My skin sizzles when I walk into her kitchen.

"How have you not passed out?" I ask.

"I know." She fans her plum-colored face. Bits of melting chocolate cling to the ends of her hair. "One more panful, and I can shut the oven off."

I help her cut the cooler trays into squares and wrap them for sale. "You're lucky you didn't get here earlier," she says. "I was pretending I was on my own baking show. I must've been delirious from the heat."

"Tell the audience, Ms. Summerlin, how you get these brownies so square?" I say, turning a spatula into a microphone.

Sylvie bats her eyes. "The secret is to cut them with *straight lines.*"

"That's ingenious," I say, still in character.

"I know. That's how I got my own cooking show." She laughs and pushes away the spatula. "How was your big mountain-climbing adventure? I've been dying to hear. Or did you have to turn back because of the rain?"

I smile at the memory of Nick and me climbing through the downpour. "Oh no, we didn't turn around. We made it to the top."

"Congratulations!" She slides the last tray into the oven.

"Something weird happened afterward, though."

"Weird? What do you mean?"

The plastic wrap sticks to my fingers. "We were in Nick's room, and he—kissed me."

"That's perfect!"

"But we've always been just friends."

She pours us glasses of ice water, and we press them to our faces for a minute. "It's great. You guys would make a cute couple."

I groan. "You did not just say 'cute couple.'"

She laughs. "Sorry. Watching you together lately—I thought maybe you liked him that way."

If Sylvie has noticed this, then has Nick? Blood rushes to my face, the last thing I need in this broiling kitchen. "Well, I don't know . . . but either way, I don't think we're 'cute.'"

"You'd be good together. You do like him, don't you?"

I'm blushing so hard that we could probably just bake the brownies on my face. "I guess."

"Then what's the problem?"

"The problem is that since it happened, I haven't heard a

word from him. He hasn't called; he hasn't texted. I think he's avoiding me."

She frowns and tests one of the trays to see if it's cool enough yet. "Why don't you call him?"

"Because I don't want to hear him stammer and try to come up with some lame excuse. . . . I mean, I could live without that humiliation."

"I can't see Nick doing that. Especially not with you."

"So why hasn't he called?"

She lifts her shoulders in a shrug. "Maybe he's been busy. You should ask him, Maggie. We could sit around guessing and try looking in a crystal ball, but it would be simpler just to talk to him."

I have my mouth open to tell her why this is impossible, when a tap on the open door interrupts us. When I see who's standing there, my jaw locks; my blood freezes. This room may be a hundred and ten degrees, but Raleigh Barringer is an ice storm.

"I came to pick up the brownies," Raleigh tells Sylvie, dangling her car keys from one sharp-nailed finger. Her eyes glide over me without changing expression, as if I'm one of the appliances. Stove, refrigerator, Maggie.

"Come on in. Raleigh, do you know Maggie?"

"We went to the same junior high," I say, my face a mask of ice.

"Oh, right, I think you told me that." Sylvie turns away to pack the wrapped brownies in a box.

I stand at the counter, moving nothing but my eyes, watching Raleigh. She merely nods in my direction. I concentrate on breathing in and out, making no sudden moves. I might as well be facing the rattlesnake all over again.

Raleigh rests one hip against the counter. Despite the temperature, her white tank top is dry. Her face is smooth, no makeup disintegrating in the heat. "I'm glad you made brownies, Sylvie. So far everyone else has made cupcakes."

"You want one of these before I wrap up the last batch?"

"No, thanks. If I ate everything I picked up today, I'd weigh twelve hundred pounds."

As if Raleigh has to worry. She's as lean as a stick of gum.

"I love your shoes," Sylvie says.

Raleigh extends her foot and studies her leather sandal. "I got them in Italy."

She always did know how to put an outfit together. Next to her I'm grubby, rumpled. "Thrift-store chic" without the chic. I flash back to seventh grade, to the whispers and giggles. Raleigh's voice breaking out above the snickers: "I can't *believe* she's wearing that. Does she pull her clothes out of a Dumpster?" Her voice rising: "What do you call that color, Maggie? Moldy liver?" And, as the next wave of laughter ebbed, her voice as penetrating as a needle but high, pseudo-sweet: "Hey, Maggie, you could be a fashion model! You could show us what homeless people are wearing this season."

I grab chocolate-coated pans and pile them in the sink. Sylvie chats with Raleigh, occasionally throwing a question my way to pull me in to the conversation, but I stick to one-word answers. I have to give Raleigh as little as possible: nothing to work with, nothing she can dig her nails into.

I'm up to my elbows in dishwater when Raleigh picks up the boxes and moves toward the door. "See you, Sylvie. I'm off to Vanessa Webb's. I hope to God she made something besides cupcakes."

Sylvie chuckles, opening the door for her. "Well, Vanessa organized this whole thing. She should know better than anyone how many cupcakes we have."

Raleigh turns toward the sink and, for the first time, looks straight at me. I hold myself up by sheer force of will, my insides shriveling with fear, while she says, "Good-bye. Maggie." A full beat between the words, every syllable clear and precise.

"Good-bye." I keep my voice steady for that one word, while under the soapy water I grip a spatula with a force that could crush coal into diamonds.

"I get the feeling you and Raleigh weren't the best of friends," Sylvie says when we're alone again.

"No."

Sylvie didn't know me in junior high. I met her last fall, the first week of sophomore year, when she walked up to me (as she walked up to practically everyone) saying, "Hi, I'm Sylvie Summerlin. I'm new here." I wondered then how she could *do* that, walk up to people as if she had a right to, never expecting anyone to sneer at her or push her away. And they didn't—sneer or push her away, that is. Sylvie has the magic of making people like her. While if I ask someone in the cafeteria to pass me a ketchup packet, they sigh and roll their eyes as if I've asked them for a lung.

I've never told her what the Raleigh Years were like for me—partly because I hate reliving them, and partly because I want to have at least one friend who doesn't see me through that lens, who doesn't know what a loser I was. It's bad enough that Nick knows, that everyone who went to my junior high knows.

"Do you want to talk about it?" Sylvie asks now, wiping the brownie pans dry.

"No, thanks." And so Sylvie goes on to tell me about some problem she's having with her girlfriend. Only I don't really hear her because all I can hear is Raleigh's voice, the threat in it: "Good-bye. Maggie."

ten

By the time I get home from Sylvie's house, in the pit of the afternoon, I still haven't heard anything from Nick. It's rare for us to go a whole day without talking; now I *know* he's avoiding me.

I can't live with my guts knotted up this way. If this is what it's like for us to try being more than friends—this tension, this uncertainty, this teetering on the verge of losing everything—then I don't need it. I'd rather stick with the friendship we already have.

Obviously, kissing was a huge mistake. Whatever attraction I thought there was—either it was only on my side, or maybe he felt it for a minute but then had second thoughts. Maybe he was just curious. After all, I am the only girl he spends much time with. But it's clear by now that we're going nowhere.

How could I forget Raleigh's words about how I make guys gag? How could I forget that no guy ever showed the slightest interest in me before Carl Gurney's "kiss-and-run," and then it was almost three years before anyone kissed me again?

Time to undo, to backspace.

If we can.

I send Nick a message: **Can we please forget it ever happened? Can we stay friends?**

Then I spend forty-five minutes pounding away at the piano, making the walls ring with stormy Beethoven.

Finally, Nick's reply comes in. When my phone chirps, I grab it and stare at the screen, the notes still echoing in the air around me.

Yes. Good idea.

And I exhale completely, for the first time in twenty-four hours.

I ride my bike over to Nick's and find him shooting baskets in his driveway. The asphalt is gooey with the heat, yet he's pounding up and down, taking shots as if the NBA championship is on the line.

I drop my bike and stand on the strip of grass that borders the driveway. Bending forward, I flip my hair up, to give my neck some air. Nick keeps dribbling and I don't interrupt, even though I think basketball is the most boring game on earth.

Every minute of it that I've ever watched—every long, long minute—is out of loyalty to Nick, who would probably wither into a catatonic strip of jerky if he had to live without it. The hoop rattles and rings; I can tell he's made the shot.

"Hey, Maggie," he pants.

I come out from under my hair. "Ready for a break?"

"In a minute."

I watch him through a veil of stray hair wisps. Nick stops at an imaginary foul line, focusing not only with his eyes but with his hands, arms, head, toes pointing to the basket. He lets the ball fly, and it sinks through the net with a *thunk*. Then he turns to me, gasping, sweat splashing from his skin onto the tar.

"God, it's hot out here," he says.

"Oh, you noticed."

"Just to the extent that my shoes are melting."

He doesn't quite meet my eyes. I don't know what to do with my hands. I itch *inside* my skin. And here I thought the awkwardness would be over with.

"Look, Maggie." He scoops the ball from the ground and straightens up. "I wanted to tell you . . . I'm sorry."

"Um, you don't have to do that." I doubt he can tell I'm blushing, because I was probably already lobster-colored from the ride over here. "It just—happened. And it's over now."

He rolls the ball around between his palms. I want to touch his hands, quiet that restless movement, get him to relax. Get us both to relax, if that's possible. But I don't know how he would take that.

It's safer not to touch.

It's better to talk about practical matters.

"I forgot to take some of my stuff home yesterday," I say. "I came to pick it up. And I brought your shirt back." I wave it at him.

"Oh, right." He bounces the ball once, twice. "You want some iced tea while you're here?"

"Yeah, okay."

I follow him inside, where he drops the ball into its usual spot beside the door, on top of a pile of grocery bags, boots, and umbrellas. He opens the refrigerator.

Sitting at the table where I've sat so many times makes me think we really will be able to return to the way things were. I know this kitchen as well as I know my own. The clean dishes piled in the drainer; the scarred cutting board where Perry often chops vegetables for stir-fry; the broken blender and the only-used-once bread maker shoved in a corner. The town map on the wall. The burn on the counter where Nick once set down a red-hot pan.

Nick plunks a spoon and a glass in front of me, and sits down with his own glass. Iced tea slops over the brim and puddles on the table.

I search for something to say, while he rubs his glass with his thumb. There's something comforting about the familiarity of his hands, his ragged nails and the dirt in the creases of his knuckles.

"So when's our next hike?" I say, scooping sugar into my glass. We might as well get back to the woods as soon as possible. Back to our old snake-fighting, mountain-climbing selves.

"I don't know."

Since when has Nick ever hesitated about getting out onto the trail? I sip my tea, bitter and sweet swirling together in my mouth. "If you don't want to hike with me anymore—" I begin, though it's like stabbing myself in the throat to say it.

"That's not it. It's just—I was thinking about another mountain. A harder one. Is that something you'd want to do?" A glance at me, the slightest flash when our eyes meet.

"Harder than Eagle? That'll be a long day." Especially if we're still off-kilter like this, our gears not quite back in sync.

"Yeah, I know. Mountains take a lot out of you, but that's kind of the point, right?" He talks to his drink, one hand wrapped around the dripping glass. "You have the summit to work for, and you put everything into the hike. . . ."

I get what he's saying. A climb will sand off the remaining sharp edges between us, will give us a place to focus all our energy. "Which mountain?" I ask.

"Crystal."

It's the one pictured on his bedroom wall, with the summit as cold and sharp as a fang. "That's in the Cinnamon Range, isn't it?"

"Yep. What do you say, Maggie?"

"I say okay."

He clinks his glass against mine, more tea slopping onto the table.

I do want to climb. I feel the same hunger, the same upward momentum, that he does.

But I have another longing to drag around with me, too. Because even though I'm relieved that he's giving me exactly what I asked for—he's treating me like a friend again—I still want more.

eleven

Whaen I get home, my mother's in bed. Her nursing shifts throw off her whole schedule, and she's often asleep when the rest of us are awake. My father's heading down into the basement workshop. "Want to join me?" he asks.

"Yes," I say, and follow him.

The workshop is mostly my dad's place (his "happy place," Mom and I joke); he built my desk and bookcase, as well as our kitchen table. But I love it, too: the clean smell of fresh wood shavings, the silkiness of sanded boards. I've built a few things myself, like the wobbly end table in our front hall, where we keep stray batteries and stacks of junk mail. My first project was an oversized "jewelry box" I made for Mom's Christmas present one year, which I inexplicably painted purple with orange flowers. She uses it to hold gloves, scarves, and umbrellas, since not even a royal family would have enough bling to fill a jewelry box that size. (At twelve, I had an underdeveloped sense of proportion and scale.) (And no eye for color.) I've since made better boxes that we've given to relatives, but my earliest attempts are too crude to inflict on anyone else.

I've actually been making my father a box for his birthday, which is coming up, but I can't work on it in front of him. Tonight, Dad plans his next job, sketching a bench my grandmother wants. While he mutters to himself, figuring height and width and depth, calculating the wood he'll need, I sort nails and screws. When we're between projects, I try to restore order to the shop. Sorting hardware is soothing, mindless work.

"How's the grid?" I ask him. I used to ask him this when I was little, when I thought of the grid almost as a living, breathing creature that he tended. I pictured the energy network as something that my father personally kept going, with the strange result that I'd often think of him whenever I flipped a switch or saw black wires sharp against a blue sky. Even though I know now that the system's a little more complicated than that, and involves more people than just my dad, "How's the grid?" has become our stock question, the equivalent of, "How are you doing?"

"It's still going," he says, which is our stock answer. He happens to be wearing a company T-shirt today: dark blue, with MID-REGIONAL POWER blazing across the front of it, in letters resembling a lightning bolt. He's offered to get me one, too (they're free), but I wouldn't be able to wear it. It would feel too bold somehow. Nick and I even have a joke about the logo: the word *POWER* is three times as big as *Mid-Regional*, and we sometimes say, "Are you feeling Mid-Regional POWERful today?"

Dad and I don't say anything more, but we don't need to. Like Nick and me, my dad doesn't talk much. My mother, on the other hand, could have a three-hour conversation with herself.

Yet when I was in junior high, Dad was the one who noticed something was wrong, who asked if everything was okay at school. Sometimes I wish I'd told him the whole truth about Raleigh and Adriana and the others. I said that kids were picking on me, but when he told me to ignore them, I didn't want to admit how bad it was. Parents are the people who brag to the world when you've mastered toilet training and the alphabet. Who wants *them* hearing you're a loser? Who wants to tell their parents that all the kids at school say you're ugly, that you stink, that everyone hates you? What if your parents squint at you when they hear that, and say, "Well, Margaret, you do smell a little, and you could stand to comb your hair more often. . . ."

After all, Mom is always saying, "Maggie, your hair is all knots." And, "That shirt is so baggy on you. Why don't we get you something a little neater?" And, "Nick is a nice boy, but you can't rely on one person all the time. You need to widen your circle of friends."

She thinks that all I have to do is wear the right clothes and smile at a few people in the cafeteria. Then they'll cluster around me, begging for my friendship, and nominate me prom queen. "Just say hello, and you'll make friends." It works for her; I've seen her leave weddings or interchurch picnics with a dozen new phone numbers even when we walked into the event hardly knowing anyone. But people don't respond to me the same way.

At school, people like Troy Truehalt and Darci Esposito look right through me. Their eyes don't even register me. Once Troy pushed past me in the lunch line—not aggressively, but as if I were a curtain he had to brush aside to reach his destination. I wonder how I look to them. Like wallpaper? Like a mannequin? Or am I completely invisible—do they not see *anything* there? I can't possibly look like a real person to them.

But at least being invisible is better than being a target.

What would Dad say if he knew I'm facing that old danger again? If I told him that Raleigh's back? I think of her slithering through Sylvie's kitchen. She didn't say much to me this morning, but her power has always been in her timing. She has always known how to strike at my weakest moments, how to make me wait for her to attack.

That waiting. I'd forgotten about it, but now it comes back to me: that feeling of never being able to exhale. Trying to watch all sides of me at once. Listening in the halls, my ears tuned for Raleigh's voice.

Naturally, she wouldn't do anything in Sylvie's house, right in front of Sylvie. I should've realized that earlier. And she's probably still getting used to being back in town. She wears that Italian trip like a velvet cape. But sooner or later, she'll slip it off and bring out the razors.

What if I could stand up to her this time?

I picture her cowering, as she was in my dream yesterday morning. I see myself responding to one of those special Raleigh-brand insults that always hit my most vulnerable spots; giving it right back to her.

Are you still in love with yourself, Raleigh? Good thing, because nobody else is.

If only I had the nerve.

I drop one last nail in a jar and step away from the bench. Dad shuffles through his wood collection, estimating what he might be able to use and what he might need to buy. As I'm heading back up the stairs, he pulls out one old board with a knot and a crack in it.

"Look at that," he says, his fingers tracing the pattern of the grain.

"You can't use that for anything, can you?"

"Probably not. But I keep thinking I'll find something to do with it. I hate to throw it away."

"It's a shame."

"It's a beautiful piece," he says, and I think he might actually like it *because* of the knot and the split.

Sunday nights are the worst: scrambling to finish the last of my homework, dreading Monday. And now, on top of that, there's the weird tension between Nick and me.

Thinking of Nick reminds me of what he said about Crystal Mountain. I dig out my guidebook and look it up.

Perhaps the most difficult day hike in the Cinnamon Range.

Wonderful.

Well, you can't accuse Nick of not aiming high enough. I read about the hazards: narrow ledges, unstable rocks, and steep drop-offs. Also snakes and bears. "What, no man-eating tigers?" I mutter to myself.

I spend some time in an online forum for local hikers, looking at the thread for Crystal Mountain.

"Those ledges!" one person has written. Another chimes in: "Forget the ledges; remember the rocks?" Which draws half a dozen replies, saying, "Oh, those ROCKS!"

I scroll down.

"That summit slope will give you vertigo." "It's not the height, it's the steepness." "No, it's the height AND the steepness!" "The rocks on the lower part are what wear you out." "I never wanted to *see* another rock after Crystal." "A couple of people died there back in 2000." "No, someone did die, but it was because he went off-trail and fell." "I heard it wasn't even a fall, it was a heart attack." "Some guy did fall, but he only broke a few bones." "They should put cables up near the summit." "No, because if they put up cables, then people who don't belong there will think they can do it."

People who don't belong there. I hope they're not talking about me.

'm still terrorizing myself with the hiking-forum posts on the dangers of Crystal Mountain when my phone beeps with a message.

I expect it to be Nick or Sylvie, but it's Adriana, with a question about the bio homework. I reread her message, searching for hidden attacks, but I can't find any dangerous subtext in **Did we have to read all of chap 4 or just as far as p. 115?**

I reply: **Page 115. Btw, where did you get my number?**

From Sylvie. Hope you don't mind. Thanks for the info!

Sylvie. Naturally. She would have no reason *not* to give out my number. And if she'd asked me first—what would I have said? How could I explain why I don't trust Adriana, without going into all the junior high drama?

I return to the Crystal Mountain descriptions, immersing myself in tales of broken legs, wild animals, and loose rocks hurtling down slopes. For all the hazards lurking there, I'd still rather take my chances on the trail than in the school halls. I text Nick: **Reading about how dangerous this mountain is. You have a strange idea of fun.**

He answers: **So you want to back out?**

I remember how it felt to stand on top of Eagle after fighting the rain and my own doubts, after pushing myself higher than I'd ever gone before. I remember the hug Nick and I shared at the top. And most of all, the energy that surged through me. The way I felt that I belonged there.

I answer Nick: **No.**

That's what I thought.

In Monday's French class, the teacher tells us to pair up for a conversation exercise. Vanessa Webb swings her chair over to my desk, even though she usually works with the girl on her other side. *"Bonjour,* Marguerite," she says.

"Bonjour." I don't know why she's chosen me today, but I'm not going to question it. At least I don't have to go through those anxious moments while everyone else couples up, wondering who will be left over.

Our assignment is to have an extremely artificial conversation about how we celebrate holidays. The book suggests that we say things like, "And your family, does it travel to the beach in the summer? There are many fine beaches."

Vanessa and I trade a few dull, clunky observations about summer vacations. I'm wishing I knew the word for "fireworks," instead of calling them "fire in the sky," when she slips off topic. Still in French, she asks me, "Nick Cleary is your friend, right?"

"*Oui*," I answer, startled, but relieved to stop straining for small talk about the Fourth of July.

She switches to English. "I thought so. I saw you two sitting together at lunch." She hesitates, running a sculpted fingernail along the spine of her French book. "Just friends?"

That question makes me swallow, sends alarm signals all the way out to my fingertips. *Good question, Vanessa.* But I simply say, "That's right."

She smiles. "Well, I'm having a party Friday night. The two of you should come. I live on the corner of Ridgway and Main. Do you know where that is?"

"Yes." I've seen her house; it dominates that corner, with its white columns and vast sweep of lawn. "But I don't know if we can make it. We're getting up early on Saturday to hike."

"You don't have to stay late. Just come for a little while. Any time after eight, all right?"

"Maybe."

"On the Fourth of July we have a picnic with much good food," she says in French, and her shift back into the assignment makes me blink.

I want to focus completely on the Saturday hike. I need to gather myself for Crystal Mountain, not only because it's a tough hike, but because it will be my first full day alone with Nick since we kissed. It will be the real test of whether we can be friends—still friends, just friends. I'd rather not have this party to worry about, blocking the entrance to my weekend like a spiked metal gate.

And what does Vanessa want with Nick, anyway?

Well, I can guess that.

Vanessa and Nick. I can't fit them together, even in my imagination. I don't think they know each other that well. What could cool, polished Vanessa, with her immaculate clothes, see in Nick the hiker, Nick the basketball player? What could he see in her?

But maybe I'm reading too much into this. Maybe she just wants a big crowd at her party, so she's asking as many people as possible. (After all, she's inviting *me*.)

I don't know. I can't figure out people at all.

After school, Nick and Luis get their basketball fix by playing an informal game with their teammates, because, apparently, that's the only way they will all survive until the season starts in a couple of months. I decide to wait for them so I can get a ride, rather than face the unknown dangers of the bus.

I lie in the grass near the court, thumbing through my mushroom guide. I know the names in this book by heart now, from false morels and liberty caps to parrot mushrooms and destroying angels. I can reel them off like a memorized poem. It fascinates me that my book labels certain mushrooms as poisonous while acknowledging that some people do eat them. The book speculates that the differences in mushroom toxicity may be due to the fact that mushrooms live off different materials in different places. They absorb what they live on.

While I consider the line between food and poison, the game provides soothing background noise: the irregular beat of the guys' feet as they run and pivot; the shuffling; the squeaking halts; the sudden thunder of the fast break.

Sylvie flops down beside me. Her eyes follow the clump of boys who migrate back and forth between the two baskets like a pendulum. "Do you think they'd let me play?" she asks. She leans forward, and her leg muscles strain, as if she has to keep herself from jumping up and joining in. She's on the girls' team during the winter.

"They're in the middle of a game now. Grudge match, very serious, out for blood. But I bet they'd let you play another time if you came at the beginning."

"Maybe I would, if I didn't have so many meetings. I'd be at Spanish club now, but it got canceled at the last minute."

Her arrival has changed the air on court. Some of the guys run faster, make bolder grabs for the ball, deal out rougher fouls. It doesn't matter that Sylvie prefers girls and they know it. She's beautiful, she's watching them, and they play harder. I, on the other hand, inspire them about as much as the concrete water fountain at the side of the court.

In books and movies, popular girls are mean, but not Sylvie. She's popular because she talks to everyone and volunteers for everything. She remembers names. She puts birthdays in her calendar and sends out personalized birthday messages. Yet she doesn't do it for the *sake* of being popular. When Sylvie asks how you are, she wants to know. She genuinely cares about whether you got that role in the play, or how long you'll have to wear the cast on your arm.

"I don't know how you keep up with everything," I say. It would exhaust me to keep track of so many people.

"Yeah, Wendy's been complaining that we don't have enough time together. Which is ironic, because the last three times I called her, *she* was busy." Sylvie scrolls through her messages. "She hasn't even texted me today."

"Listen, Sylvie—did you hear anything about a party at Vanessa Webb's this weekend?"

"On Friday? Yeah. I can't go because that's the night of my cousin's wedding." She looks up from her phone. "I got a new dress for it, but now I'm thinking it's a mistake. It's garnet, and it kind of washes me out." She tilts her head and studies me. "It would look perfect on you, though, with your dark hair and eyes. Why don't you wear brighter colors?"

Because I'm just trying to get through high school without anyone noticing, I think. "I don't know."

"The skirt would be the right length for you, too. If my legs were in as good shape as yours, I'd wear skirts all the time."

I look down at my jeans. Raleigh always said my knees were too knobby, so I hide them as much as possible. But maybe hiking has built up my leg muscles?

Or maybe Sylvie's only being nice.

She scrolls through her messages again, frowning. "Wendy didn't text me yesterday, either."

But my mind is on the party, on trying to prepare for it any way I can. "What do you know about Vanessa?"

"She's on a couple of committees with me—she organized the bake sale. And she helps me out with math sometimes." Sylvie starts typing. "I'm going to see if I can get ahold of Wendy."

I was hoping to hear something juicier about Vanessa— anything to indicate she's less than perfect. Even just an embarrassing nickname. But Sylvie isn't much of a gossip, even if she knew anything scandalous about Vanessa.

I chew on the sweet white end of a grass stem, thinking about Vanessa and her invitation, while Sylvie tries to reach Wendy.

The game breaks up. After Nick and Luis suck down water from the fountain, they join us. Even though I didn't watch much of the game or track the score, I can tell they won by all the strutting and grinning. "Good rebounding, Luis," Sylvie says.

"*Somebody* has to get the rebounds." Luis pokes an elbow into Nick.

"Hey, I don't need to get that close to the basket to make a shot."

"The only reason you take all those outside shots is that you can't make a layup."

"The reason I take all those outside shots is that I make them."

And on they go, their bickering even louder and happier than usual because they were both on the winning team. I used to hate this kind of back-and-forth; it seemed nasty to me. And perhaps there is an edge to it, some real competition between them, but now I think this is the way Nick and Luis show how tight they are—maybe the only way they can show it.

Sylvie says good-bye. I get in the car with the guys, the air thick with testosterone. They take apart the winning plays, analyzing how they broke down the other team's defenses. If they could bring this much insight to the actions and motives of world leaders, they'd have lifetime jobs in the State Department. They talk basketball nonstop until we drop off Luis.

I get in the front seat. "Can you maybe forget about the game for a minute?"

Nick laughs. "I can try, but I'm not promising anything."

"Guess who wants to see you at her party Friday night."

"Tilman?"

Mrs. Tilman is the school principal. "Ha. No, Vanessa Webb."

"Oh yeah?"

"Do you know her? She invited both of us, but it was obvious you were the main attraction."

"We had the same English class last year." Nick pauses, taking a sharp corner. "Do you want to go?"

"Not really."

"It could be fun."

I suck in my breath. "Are you saying *you* want to go?"

"I don't know. Maybe. Why not?"

"It's not exactly our crowd."

He laughs again. "We have a crowd?"

"Well, no—that's my point."

We go to Nick's house and slog through our homework, taking turns at his computer. I get it first while he showers off his basketball sweat. Afterward, we lie on his bed together, watching TV. I'm careful to leave several inches of space between us, preserving our just-friends pact.

During one of the commercials, I bring up the question that's been bothering me since our ride home. "Why do you want to go to Vanessa's party?"

It's easier to ask those kinds of questions when you're both staring at something besides each other.

"How come you *don't* want to?" he asks after a long pause.

"It'll be so crowded. And you know I don't like to drink."

"You don't have to," he says. "I won't be drinking much, either, since I'll be driving."

"I still don't see why you want to go. You're not usually that big on—how shall I say this—*people*." Other than me, Nick's social circle consists mainly of guys who have one thing in common: they play basketball. Not that they don't party. But a few beers after a game is a lot different from being invited, several days in advance, to go to someone's house. I'm trying to picture Nick, in his boots and holey jeans, stomping into Vanessa's tree-shaded, columned house.

"I want to get out for a change." He taps the mattress. "Come on, we'll both go. And if you stay over here that night, we can drive out to Crystal first thing Saturday."

"I could stay over without going to the party."

"True. You don't have to go if you don't want to."

Well, if he's determined to go, I'm not going to sit home preparing for my solitary future of having tea parties for my ten cats. I don't want him to leave me completely behind while he tries out the junior-class party scene. "No, I'll come with you," I say. "Someone has to keep you out of trouble."

"Good." He shifts on the bed beside me, and I can hear him breathing. He picks up the remote, because a commercial has come on. Nick refuses to watch two minutes of advertising if he can use that time to click through fifty other channels instead.

"Nick," I say, keeping my voice light, "people don't actually die from watching commercials."

"You mean nobody's died *yet*."

My eyes stray from the flashing screen to the map and photo on the wall: the jagged tooth of the Crystal Mountain summit, higher and sharper than that of Eagle. On Crystal, we'll be alone together—back to our old selves, our old bond, the special world we've created with and for each other. If only I can get through this party first.

thirteen

After school on Thursday, Nick and Luis play another basketball game while I do homework in the grass near the court. The guys play hard, shoving and laughing, pivoting, faking one another out. Nick and Luis revel in it, pushing for every edge, striving to get the ball exactly where they want it even if they end up bruised. I still prefer hiking, where there's nothing to fight, and there's only the trail to test yourself against.

Along with the occasional snake and rainstorm.

As the fall sports teams finish their practices, the football players, cross-country runners, and soccer players straggle back toward the building. The guys on the basketball court end their game. They cluster around the water fountain, jostling and joking, and I gather my books.

Raleigh Barringer pauses at the fountain on her way back from the soccer field, her dark hair pulled back in a ponytail.

The guys move aside for her; I wish I knew why. If I got up for a drink, they'd tell me to get in line.

After drinking, she straightens and says to Luis, "Nice shorts, Morales." Luis likes bright colors—today it's electric orange.

He grins and turns his back to her. Over his shoulder, he says, "Enjoy the view. It's not the shorts that count; it's what's *in* the shorts that counts."

Everyone laughs, including Raleigh, who says, "Will you be showing us *that* next?"

"If you insist." He reaches for his waistband.

Half the guys groan or say, "No! Don't take 'em off!" while the other half hoot and urge him on. "Give the people what they want!"

Luis pulls his waistband down maybe an inch while he watches Raleigh, both of them laughing, him daring her to tell him to stop. But she crosses her arms and stands her ground, and even taps her foot with mock impatience.

"Nobody needs to see that." Nick elbows Luis. "Come on, you want a ride home or not?"

"Aw, Nick, there you go, spoiling all the fun," Raleigh says.

My nerves prickle at the sound of his name in her voice. Nick and Luis didn't go to our junior high. How has she learned everyone's names so quickly?

"That's my job," Nick says.

"You got that right," Luis says.

"Just for that, you can ride on the roof," Nick tells him.

When they pass Raleigh, she says, "See you later," in a way that makes it sound like a real promise, instead of the throwaway line it usually is.

As Nick and Luis come toward me, the other guys cluster around her. "Say something in Italian, Raleigh."

She obliges, syllables rolling off her tongue like music.

"What's that mean?" They hang on her words, tantalized. She draws them toward her like fish on a line.

And then she snaps the line, laughing.

"It means, 'I want to buy some cheese.'" With that, she waves at them and walks away.

I wait until after we've dropped off Luis to ask Nick, "How do you know Raleigh?"

"She's in my gym class."

I fight not to ask, because I know it sounds paranoid, but I can't stop myself. "Do you talk to her a lot?"

"No." He stops for a light. "Maggie, she's no threat to you. Junior high's over."

"That's what I thought . . . until she showed up here." It's bad enough to see her in the halls, in the cafeteria. But it's worse to see her at Sylvie's, or to watch her flirt with Luis and Nick at the water fountain. It's like she's infiltrating my circle, small as it is. Is that her plan—to cut me off from my friends, the way a wolf cuts a weak deer from the herd?

If anyone should understand, it's Nick. Because our friendship started in the depths of the Raleigh Years.

Nick went to Eastern District Junior High, and I went to West End. At first, we were just two kids whose mothers were friends. Back then, my mom had to work a lot of afternoon shifts and Phoebe didn't, so I went to Nick's house after school.

We sometimes made halfhearted stabs at our homework, but mostly we raided the kitchen. One afternoon in seventh grade, I was eating cookies. They were chocolate mint cookies with a fudgy coating, and as I rolled that richness over my tongue I wondered how it could be so good while the rest of my life was so horrible. And I began to cry. I wasn't sobbing outright, but I knew by the sudden salt in my mouth, and the way the kitchen blurred, that tears were creeping down my face.

"What's wrong?" Nick asked.

I shook my head. Nick didn't push, but he didn't walk away from it, either. He could have shrugged it off or changed the subject. But he waited for me to tell him.

"It's those bitches at school," I said at last, and rubbed the wetness off my face. I licked chocolate crumbs from my teeth.

He'd probably already gathered that I was on the fringes at my school, but Nick didn't worry about things like that, about popularity and the social pecking order. Even if we'd gone to the same school, he might not have seen everything that was happening. His other friends were boys, boys he played basketball with. Sometimes I was amazed at how the guys at school seemed to live in a totally different world from the girls. They didn't know much about our fights and gossip, our alliances and broken friendships.

"Raleigh Barringer and Adriana Lippold worst of all," I said. "I wish they would die."

Nick played with a twist tie someone had left on the table, bending it, knotting it.

"They never stop picking on me. They go after me in the hall, in the girls' room, everywhere. They have a page about me online. They had another one before, and I complained to the host site and got it taken down, but they started up the same thing somewhere else. They make up lies about me. They tell me I'd be better off dead."

Nick twisted the tie into a corkscrew shape, a helix.

"I've been reading about these poisonous mushrooms, and I keep imagining how I could sneak toadstools into their lunch and have them die in front of the whole school, their faces turning blue and their muscles cramping up—"

The words spilled out. I seldom talked this way because people (especially adults) always acted so shocked, so disapproving, if I said anything angry. But Nick leaned forward.

"Do poison mushrooms really turn your face blue?"

"I don't know," I admitted. "The book doesn't say."

"But it tells you which ones are poison?"

"Yeah. Well, not all of them. Some of them, people aren't sure. And some people eat mushrooms that other people call poisonous."

He was still leaning forward, so I showed him the book. We paged through it, searching for all the fungi marked poisonous. Picturing the death throes of Raleigh and Adriana gave me a coziness in my stomach, even better than the cookies.

Or that's what I thought then. Now I think that what made me feel better was the fact that Nick listened to me, that he understood, that he didn't tell me I was awful for thinking this way.

"You know I'm not serious," I told him, suddenly alarmed at how much I'd said, when the time came for me to go home. Would he tell his mother—or even worse, mine? Would he rat me out, get me expelled from school for threatening other students? "I wouldn't really poison anyone."

"Yeah, I know that," he said.

My skin was damp with nervousness by then, my gut churning. Raleigh and Adriana told me a thousand times a day that they wanted me to die. They threatened to break my arms, burn me, and scar my skin. They told me I should kill myself. And yet when I fantasized about poisoning them, I felt guilty.

The worst thing Raleigh and the other girls did was to plant that lump of coal inside me, the shame of believing I was the wrong one, wrong in every way. After all, there must be something wrong with me *or why else would they be picking on me?*

But Nick never told anyone what I'd said. I didn't know why he understood how I felt. I only knew that Nick did understand, and from then on he was not just the guy whose house I had to stay at while my mother worked. From then on, we were friends.

So I don't know how he can say that Raleigh isn't a real threat to me. I open my mouth to argue with him, when his phone goes off. Beethoven's Seventh rings out like a bad omen, a warning.

Nick groans. "Will you get that? Tell him I'm driving." He shoves the phone at me.

"Why don't you let it go to voice mail?"

"He hates voice mail."

Only Nick's father could try to deny a fact of life as ingrained as voice mail, but I answer the phone. "Hello?"

"Who's this?" Nick's father booms.

"It's Maggie, Dr. Cleary. Nick's driving right now."

"He couldn't pull over? Never mind. Tell him I can't take him to dinner tonight after all. My idiot post-doc screwed up a month's worth of data, and I'm going to be working all night."

"Okay."

"But tell him to text me about how he's doing in history. I want to know what's going on there."

"I will."

"Good. Thank you, Margaret." Dr. Cleary hangs up before I can say good-bye. Or anything else.

I pass on the message to Nick, who says, "That breaks my heart, that I can't spend the whole night getting grilled about my history grade."

"Aw, don't worry, Nick. I can grill you about your history grade if you want."

"Sounds like a fun night."

"Seriously, though—if you want help, I could work with you. I got an A in Connard's class last year."

"Okay. Thanks."

That night, when we're going over the causes of the Great Depression at his kitchen table, I lean over to point out a date on the time line in his book. When he looks up from the page, we're eye to eye, our faces close enough to kiss. He draws back, and as soon as he does, I do, too, so I'm not left leaning in toward him as if I expect something. We can barely look at each other for another half hour or so.

And it's like a slap, because before last weekend, that awkwardness was never there. As much as I wish he would've leaned in toward me just now, I would settle for his not springing away from me as if I've scalded him.

He gets up to hunt for something to eat, and trips over some books he piled behind his chair, knocking them across the floor. He says, "For my next trick, I'll use my athletic skill to scale Crystal Mountain."

We laugh, and I help him pick up the books, and we ease back into our old selves. Yet I wonder how many times we're going to stumble over moments like these, how long it's going to take to get all the way back to normal—if normal is even possible.

fourteen

Nick and I are on our way to Vanessa's party. My nerves tighten when he turns onto Ridgway, the curving road leading to her house. I can tell that he has just showered—the dampness of his hair, the scent of soap—and it seems strange for the two of us to be out after dark, as clean as if it's morning.

I'm chewing a cinnamon candy because someone once told me it was better for your breath than mint, and my shoulders are cold. I shouldn't have worn a shirt this thin, but I saw the same shirt on a girl at school, so I figured it would fit in at the party. If only Sylvie hadn't been preoccupied with her cousin's wedding tonight, I could've asked her what to wear. As it was, I texted her about forty times today.

I spent the afternoon playing the darkest, most powerful piano pieces I could find, in the hope that it would give me confidence. When I was able to play my final song without a single mistake, I told myself it was a sign that the party would go all right. I'm trying to hold on to the music, but already it's slipping away, drowned out by the growl of the car engine.

Nick parks on the street behind a long line of cars. Every light in Vanessa's house is on. My fingers go cold as we walk up to her front door. Music pulses behind that door, a faint thump I feel in my feet and deep inside my ears. I tell myself, "Fun, this is supposed to be fun," in a desperate attempt to lighten up. But I can't shake the feeling I'm walking into a trap, a prison.

With this attitude, I ought to be the queen of the party. Fun-seeking people always flock to the girl wearing the grimace of endurance! If only I could channel Sylvie.

Nick tries the door, and it's unlocked. We step into a room smelling of sweat and beer, crammed with bodies. The music makes my fillings vibrate. Luis is already there, beer in hand, in a bright green shirt that reminds me of lime Popsicles. He hugs me while I decide it's a good omen that he's the first person I see. Maybe this won't be so bad.

And then two guys from the basketball team drag Nick off somewhere. A girl grabs Luis's hand and dances away with him, and already I am alone. Five minutes into the party, in the center of the room, I've become the wallflower.

Blend in, I tell myself, and begin to walk. I have nowhere to go, but walking gives the illusion that I do.

I sit on the kitchen counter, nursing a Coke. I know everyone in the room—that is, I know their names. Phil Warren is making out with Darci Esposito in front of the fridge. Troy Truehalt hangs over the sink, his face a horrible shade of chartreuse. Janie Fletcher is nearly falling out of her dress, laughing at whatever Iggy Conant is saying.

Raleigh and Adriana stand in the corner, striking poses. Adriana flashes her teeth at everyone who passes; her squeal rises above every other noise in the room. She talks in exclamation points. *Bryan! It's so good to see you! Hi, Cody! Hey, Iggy! Come here a second!*

Out in the living room, someone must be chugging, judging by the shouts of "Drink! Drink!"

I text Sylvie, even though I know she can't answer in the middle of a wedding. She'll get the messages later. For now, I'm just saving my sanity by sending one after the other:

Help! I'm trapped!

Vanessa's kitchen floor has a very interesting pattern. Not that I am bored or anything.

How many decibels does it take for music to break windows?

At a party is it considered impolite to take a box of Cheez-Its out of the cabinet and fling them everywhere like snow? Or is this considered festive? Not that anyone here *cough Shayna Burton cough* has done any such thing. Should I pick the crackers out of my hair now, or wear them like ornaments?

I could keep this up all night. And, unless Nick or Luis reappears, I may have to.

Lissa Carpenter joins Adriana and Raleigh. The main thing I always remember about Lissa is how she once said she wished she had cancer so she could get skinny. I sip my Coke and watch them from the sides of my eyes. I know better than to look directly at them. Lissa and Adriana bend toward each other, murmur, giggle, run nervous hands through their hair, wave their drinks around, pull at the hems of their shirts. They are never still for a moment. Raleigh is quieter, leaning back against the wall with an amused smile on her face that says this place is *okay,* but it's no Venetian palazzo.

Into the kitchen swaggers Ethan Crannick. In eighth grade, egged on by Raleigh, he used to make retching noises at me. He hasn't done it in a couple of years, but every time I see him, I spend the first few seconds expecting it, that thunderous gagging that used to turn heads in the hall.

He walks over to Adriana, who touches his sleeve and glows.

It's all like watching a play. Except that in this play, I might be dragged up onstage and humiliated at any moment. I try not to make any sudden moves. *I am one with this kitchen counter,* I tell myself.

Raleigh glances at me, then whispers to Lissa and Adriana and Ethan. They all snicker, and I have to stop myself from jumping off the counter and running out of the house.

That's how her campaign against me started in junior high: with whispers. Suppressed giggles. The hiss of words I couldn't quite hear. Heads averted, eyes rolling to the corners of their sockets to see if I noticed. To make sure I noticed. Then Raleigh's voice breaking out above the snickers: "Maggie picks her nose and eats it!" "Maggie walks like a gorilla!" "Maggie *smells* like a gorilla!" "Maggie tried to sell her body on Washington Street, but nobody would buy it!"

I can't hear Raleigh now, but I can imagine what she might be saying. *I won't take it this time,* I tell myself. I hunt for words to use against her, preparing for attack. *Raleigh, didn't we already get rid of you once? What terrible thing did we do to Italy to make them send you back to us?* It doesn't matter that it's not the most brilliant insult ever invented. She doesn't expect me to say *anything,* so if I can speak up at all, it's better than nothing.

I'm grateful that at least she's sticking firmly with her own group. Knowing that she's in clubs with Sylvie and gym class with Nick, having seen her flirt with Luis, I've been worried that she might try to peel my friends away from me. But she hasn't made any moves along that front, and tonight she's surrounded by her own friends, with no sign of stepping more than six inches away from them. Her battle plan must be something else.

Raleigh, Lissa, Adriana, and Ethan move into the hall together, without another glance in my direction. Now I'm not sure if they were talking about me at all.

I never know. Just in case, I don't let myself relax.

Luis leads a line of dancers into the already-packed kitchen. He moves as smoothly here as he does on the basketball court.

He beckons to me, but I shake my head. Years of piano lessons taught me to find a beat, so I'm not worried about the rhythm, just about trying to move freely in front of everyone.

The dancers make a circuit around the kitchen, and this time when Luis passes me, he grabs my hand and pulls me off the counter. I'm swept into the tide, adjusting my dancing to match the motion of the others.

For a few minutes, it's beautiful, the way we all move together. I belong; I'm in tune with everyone around me. We lock into the beat as if it's keeping us alive.

Luis abandons himself to the music, pumping his hips with no shame or self-consciousness, and I wish I could let myself go like that. But underneath, my internal alarm system's on alert. Some part of me stands back and watches the people around me for danger signs: smirks, superior glances, whispers. I don't see any, but I shrink back toward the counter, anyway.

When he sees me slipping away, Luis stretches a hand toward me. It's an invitation, and I take it, dancing there for as long as he holds me, trying to remember the last time I felt so welcome in a crowd. The heat in the room is suffocating, moisture running down the steamed windows, but somehow it urges us on, fuels us all.

I read Luis's moves—I seem to read them even before he makes them—and he reads mine, and we're never out of step with each other. It's like a conversation, only easier.

But other girls surround him. They approach him from all sides, and I can see how badly they'd like me to leave the floor.

I edge away, and the group swallows up Luis. I return to my perch on the countertop while the dancers flow back toward the living room.

Nick enters the kitchen and leans against the counter next to me. "Is this party everything you dreamed it would be?" I ask him.

He shrugs and tilts up his cup of beer.

"How many drinks is that for you?" I wouldn't care, except he's driving.

"First one."

Vanessa, whose back is to us, looks over her shoulder. Her eyes meet Nick's, and they hold that gaze so long I want to wave my hand in front of his face to make sure he's still conscious. I try to read the look that passes between them: heat, or challenge, or a question . . . all of that, but mostly a question. *What question? What is with them?*

Nick looks away first, and Vanessa turns back to her circle of friends. Nick takes another swallow of beer.

"Why don't we get going?" I say.

"I want to show you something first."

"Aw, Nick, I bet you say that to all the girls." The line is out of my mouth before I can check myself. It's the kind of joke I would've made without thinking just a few weeks ago. But with what has happened between us, it takes on a new bite that instantly makes me wish I could take it back.

He doesn't react, though, still intent on whatever he wants to show me. "Seriously. Come on."

He leaves his beer on the counter, takes my hand, and leads me through clumps of people. The heat of the room laps against our skin. Nick leads me down an empty hall and pushes open a door. I'm about to ask him what we're doing when an eerie, luminous glow from inside the room dries up all the words on my tongue.

We're surrounded by bluely glowing aquariums. Soft motors chuff, and the aquariums bubble, but otherwise it's silent. The reflected ripples on the bare walls make me feel that I'm underwater, too, while the fish glide past me. They flick their fins, shimmer, and probe the glass with tiny mouths.

"What is this place?" I whisper.

"Vanessa's brother likes fish."

"'Likes' may be an understatement." I walk past the tanks, fighting the urge to make swimming motions, expecting the air in here to be as heavy as water. The blue light tranquilizes me.

Nick stands behind me while I study one tank, its mossy plants and jewel-bright fish creating a tiny secret kingdom. He's so close that his breath warms my neck, and that warmth travels through me, tickling my nerves. The party has faded to a background murmur. We are alone.

We've been alone before, but there's a stirring between us now, something charged. If I turn, we'll be face-to-face.

I stay right where I am, relishing how near he is, pretending I'm going to turn around any minute. Pretending he'll lean into me, that our mouths will meet. Knowing all the time that I can't risk it. Reminding myself that just last night, he recoiled when we got too close. I wish I could stop thinking about kissing him, stop imagining it every time we're alone. *Been there, failed at that.* I wish the daydreaming part of my brain would get the message.

I keep facing the glowing aquariums. This room is its own world. The silence builds and builds until I have to break it. "I love this place."

He laughs softly. "I knew you would."

"How did you even find it?"

"Vanessa showed me."

His words bump against me like a finger tapping the wall of a fish tank. Something that I can't fully see ripples around me.

"Vanessa showed you?"

"Yeah."

"Since when are you such great friends?"

He doesn't answer.

"What's going on with you, Nick?" I turn my back on the aquariums, to see his expression, but his face in here is mostly dark. Silvery-blue light touches his nose and lips and chin. The electricity in the room has turned dangerous, the kind of spark that snaps and stings. "I saw the look you two gave each other out there."

"What look?" he says.

"When we were in the kitchen."

"I don't know what you're talking about."

"Oh, come on. You were practically slurping each other up with your eyes."

He stretches a finger toward the glass of one tank. He doesn't tap it, but runs his finger along the outside to see if the fish will follow it. "Nothing's going on with me and Vanessa."

"Yet."

I'm guessing here, but his pause confirms it.

"I don't know," he says.

I don't know. Not, "Nothing's going to happen." Not, "You're imagining things, Maggie." My world slides sideways, flips me over, and all the blood rushes to my head.

The door bangs open, and two people stumble into the room, laughing. It's Darci and Phil. "Ooh, someone's already here," Darci giggles. I worry that they might lurch into the tanks and break them. But they fall onto a futon that must belong to Vanessa's brother.

"We were just leaving," Nick says.

"Don't let us push you out," Darci says, but Phil's already kissing her with the loud, wet, stomach-turning smacks of a Saint Bernard.

In the dark hall, I tell Nick, "I want to get out of here." And this time he doesn't argue with me.

We're in the car before Nick speaks again. As we take the curves of Ridgway, he says, "What's your problem with Vanessa?"

"I don't have a problem with Vanessa."

"It sure seems like it." Nick's eyes stay fixed on the road, his hands at perfect nine-and-three on the wheel, as if I'm a DMV examiner giving him a road test.

"It just takes some getting used to. You haven't had a girlfriend before, and—"

"Did you think I was never going to?" he cuts in, his voice defensive. I swear I don't understand what's happening between us tonight.

"It's not that." But I realize he's right, sort of. Not the way he means it—I never thought he *couldn't* find a girlfriend—but somehow I thought he wouldn't want to. I guess I've imagined the two of us going along like this forever, always being closer to each other than we are to anyone else. Even when he didn't want to take our kiss any further, I never imagined him putting another girl in my place.

I twist the ends of my hair. "You're my best friend." I clear my throat, still winding hair around my fingers. "I don't want that to change. I want us to keep hiking and—"

"Don't worry," he says, his voice rough, almost impatient. "We're still friends."

Friends with a mountain to climb tomorrow, I remind myself. But I'm not sure how I'm going to climb it with this new Nick, with the shadow of Vanessa between us.

fifteen

W e're halfway up Crystal Mountain. The day has turned unseasonably hot, a last blazing gasp of summer. Sun bakes the rocks. Moisture collects on my scalp, under the straps of my backpack, and at the bottom edges of my bra. A hot wind swirls around the boulder where Nick and I sit munching fist-fuls of trail mix. We've climbed high enough that the valley below us has shrunk to toy size, with miniature trees and matchstick light poles and a steely ribbon of river. But there's still plenty of mountain above us.

"I should've brought my own trail mix. Without *raisins*," I say.

"Yeah, can you leave something for me besides raisins? I'm going to take all the ones you're picking out and stick them in your backpack when you're not looking."

We squabble, laughing, the way we have on a dozen other hikes. On the outside, it's as if we're back to normal.

But all morning, the party has loomed between us. I went

there worrying about Raleigh, but came out worrying about Vanessa. The fact that Nick's been smiling to himself all morning hasn't helped. Everything I say feels like I'm pushing words against a barrier between us. But I keep trying.

"I need fuel," I say. "Look at those ledges ahead of us."

"Up there? We can do that."

I gulp water and hop off our boulder, whose surface is starting to burn me even through my shorts. "Well, let's go. Crystal isn't going to climb itself."

"If it did, that would sure save *us* a lot of trouble." Nick stuffs the bag of trail mix into his pack. I stretch and shake out my legs, waiting for him to buckle his pack straps.

We pick our way over ridges of burning rock. Skinny, twisted trees grip the mountain with their roots, but none of them casts enough shade to shield us. I can almost feel my skin reddening, and we stop at the bottom of the next steep section to slather on sunscreen.

We can't see our own faces, so we usually smooth off the excess gobs of sunscreen for each other. Sliding my finger down the side of his cheek, closing my eyes as he wipes my forehead, I tell myself it doesn't mean anything. I rub my hand on the bottom of my T-shirt, wishing I could rub off my discomfort as well. It's so much easier to keep Nick in the friend category when we're not stroking each other's faces. . . .

I need to concentrate.

For the first time, looking up at the narrow ledges where we'll be climbing on the very rim of the mountain, I shiver. I'm not exactly afraid of heights, but I'll be putting my feet inches from a thousand-foot drop. That could make anyone gulp.

The blazes, paint blotches marking the rock, lead up into the sky. They wind around the left side of the mountain, where there's a rim just wide enough to walk on. We'll have rock rising on our right, a steep drop-off to our left, and then we'll reach a point where we go up the face of Crystal. From here it looks blank and sheer and impossible, but I know that when we get there, we'll find bumps and imperfections in the rock that will allow us to move up. Still—

"I forgot to bring my wings," I tell Nick. When in doubt, make a joke.

"Didn't I tell you you'd need them today?"

He leads, and I ignore the quivering in my legs. *Be strong*, I tell myself, moving one step at a time, drawing comfort from the solid rock on my right as the edge of the world creeps ever closer on my left. The empty air over there sings with the strange magnetic pull that heights have, an invisible downward pressure.

Gusts of wind smash into my face. They batter the wall beside me, ricochet and try to sweep me over the side. My stomach tightens. But I reach the base of the next section, where Nick waits. He pulls out his phone and snaps a picture of the trail upward, then turns to take a couple of the view below.

"How come you're doing that?" I ask. Both of us usually prefer to keep hikes inside ourselves, rather than taking pictures we'll never look at again. We've always said that pictures don't begin to tell the story of what trails are really like. And when I think of myself scrutinizing the picture of Perry on the summit of Eagle, unable to get any real answers from it, I know it's true.

"Vanessa asked me to, so she could see what it's like out here. She actually wanted to come with us, but I thought this would be too rough for a beginner's hike."

"When did she ask you that?"

"She called me last night, after we got back from the party."

Vanessa called him after the party? I wait for more details, but he doesn't give any, and it makes me queasy to ask. Not only would it feel like I'm prying, chiseling at the barrier between us that has just gotten thicker . . . but I'm not entirely sure I *want* to hear the details.

Instead, I turn to look up at the section ahead of us. Now we can see that Crystal's smooth wall isn't smooth after all, just as I suspected. The steep, slick sections are interspersed with narrow ledges.

"Ready?" Nick says, grinning as if he's earned a spot on the NBA All-Star team. Perhaps he hasn't noticed how *high* we are.

"Sure," I say, to convince myself that I am. I try to find our old bond, to tap into our mutual belief that we can handle any trail, but I still feel cut off from him. Almost as if I'm alone up here.

Nick moves up the rock, finding ripples and notches, sometimes using his hands at the steeper spots. Behind us the void yawns; the wind howls out of it. I take an extra minute to gather myself before I follow Nick.

Every step takes me higher into uncertainty, higher into the unknown. My legs and fingers tremble. I've never felt this scared on a trail before—not even in the rain last week. I search inside myself for the inner steel I'll need to make this climb, for the joy I've felt on trails before. I think of those T-shirts from my dad's company. And how, at the moment, I'm not feeling my Mid-Regional POWER.

A hawk shrieks, its voice bouncing off the walls of rock, its screech like a cold talon slicing down the back of my neck.

Don't slip, I tell myself, my mouth dry.

And now I can't stop thinking about slipping, tumbling down the trail. Flying off the mountain, crashing all the way to the valley floor.

All the mistakes I could make, all the missteps I must not take, fight for attention in my head—so many of them that I have no brain cells left for climbing.

I stop and hold on to the rock, my stomach feeling like I've swallowed live frogs. And for all the air up here, I can't get any into my lungs.

I'm stuck.

"Maggie!" Nick calls. He's somewhere above me, but I can't look up. I can't look anywhere but at the rock right in front of my face. I fix on it, convinced that this is the only thing keeping me alive. If I look away, I'll die.

"Maggie, you okay?"

I close my eyes.

I know this feeling of utter helplessness—I had it every day back in junior high—but it's never happened on a trail before. I've always been able to talk myself through tough spots. Right now my inner voice only screams, *We're gonna die!!!* Which is not helping at all.

Boots scrape against rock, the sounds descending toward me. Nick must be coming back.

"What's wrong?" He's right above me now.

"I can't move," I say, my voice high and thin.

"Why? Are you hurt?"

"No, it's—vertigo or something."

"It's okay," he says.

I want to believe him. But my hands and feet cling to the mountain as if magnetized.

"Can you move one of your feet?" he asks.

"No," I pant.

"Just one foot."

I open my eyes. With three of my limbs hanging on to the mountain, I move my right foot. My throat closes when that foot leaves solid ground, but when I put my foot down again, a little higher than it was before, I think, *Okay, I can move now.*

"Now one hand," Nick says.

My right hand inches up, confidence trickling back into my veins. And then a gust of wind hits us, blowing my hair into my face.

I close my eyes. The hawk screams again, and I can't control my limbs. The voice in my head switches back to, *You can't do this! You can't!*

"You're doing fine," Nick says. A lie. But I love him for that lie.

He climbs down beside me and rests a hand on my back, which is soaked in sweat.

Panic clutches the controls of my brain, jerks the steering wheel. "I have to go down. Now." Something in me kicks loose, and my limbs move.

I finally break free of the mountain—not to climb upward, but to retreat.

I scramble down the slope on legs that don't feel fully connected to my body. "Maggie, hold on," Nick calls. And since I've hit a flat spot, I wait. But some internal clock urges me to escape, as if there's a time bomb buried on Crystal. I twist my body to face him, but my feet are still pointed down the mountain.

"We can do this climb," he says. "Take a breath. We can go as slow as you want."

"I need to get down." I raise my hand to brush a loose strand of hair from my face, and nearly poke myself in the eye.

His eyes follow my trembling fingers, and he doesn't say any more. He follows me down.

🍃 🍃 🍃

"What happened up there?" Nick asks when we're back at his car, standing by the open doors, waiting for the pent-up heat to dissipate.

"I don't know." I can hear the tears in my voice, and I tamp them down. All I need, to lose any last scrap of self-respect, is to start blubbering. It's not like I broke a leg. "It was a—panic attack or something."

"But why?"

"I don't know." How can I explain the swirling inside my brain? The feeling of isolation, the sense that I'd lost half my hiking team? Nick is here with me. Even if a piece of his mind seems to be with Vanessa, it's unfair of me to resent that. And how can I explain that the shrieks of the hawk felt like judgment, sounded like a voice screaming that I couldn't do it— exactly like every other screaming voice I carry in my head?

Nick's staring at me, but I can't meet his eyes. "Are you okay?" he asks.

"Yeah. I'll be fine. I'm sorry."

"You don't have to apologize."

Nick slides into the driver's seat and starts the engine. I get in, and we roll down the windows. The car is a hand-me-down from Perry, and the air-conditioning is broken.

"So we have a little glitch in our mountain-climbing plan," I say, trying to be cheerful. "The glitch of me not being able to climb a mountain." I raise my water bottle for a sip.

"You'll do it. You made it up Eagle, right? Crystal will just take practice. Lots of people don't make it on the first try."

First try? I nearly choke on my water as I realize: *good Lord, he expects me to go up there again.*

Hiking is one of the few things I'm good at, one of the few things I know how to do. Even before I met Nick and Perry, I already loved the patch of woods behind my house. I knew trees better than I knew people. I would stroke the chalky white bark of birches and marvel at how trembling aspens really did tremble. After the mitten-shaped leaves of sassafras turned scarlet in the fall, I pressed them between dictionary pages.

When Perry brought us out onto the trails, I discovered a new home outdoors—with rock and waterfalls, secret pockets of ferns and moss. The back country has always been a good place, a place I belong.

Until today, it's never thrown me a challenge I couldn't meet.

I have to fight to keep from veiling my face with my own long hair, as if that could hide me from Nick, as if sheer will-power could make me disappear. Because even though he seems to think this is just a temporary setback, I'm not so sure. I don't understand what's happening to me, or what I can believe in now.

sixteen

When I get home from Crystal, I head down to the basement to work on the wooden box I'm making for Dad's birthday.

A couple of days ago, I put on the hinges. Now I open and close the lid, marveling at the smoothness of the motion. The lid isn't crooked; the hinges don't balk or wiggle. I made one of these for my piano teacher when he stopped teaching me, as a good-bye present, and that time it took me forever to get the hinges right. At least there's something in the world that I'm getting better at.

Thinking of my piano teacher reminds me of what he used to tell me when I had trouble with a piece of music: go slow, break it down, practice it over and over.

And then I realize that's exactly what Nick was coaching me to do, when he told me to move one foot at a time, one hand at a time. If I'd stayed with it, if I hadn't insisted on turning around, would I have broken through?

Maybe. I'm not sure I could have forced myself to stay in that terror. Even now, with no mountain under my feet, nervousness tickles the back of my throat, threatens to trigger my gag reflex. I swallow.

I put a coat of stain on Dad's box and then send Sylvie a series of texts describing my panic on Crystal, asking what's wrong with me, asking if she thinks I'll get over it. When she doesn't answer, I call her.

"Oh—Maggie," she says. "I got your messages. I'm sorry you had such a bad day."

I launch into the story again, trying to make her understand the height and steepness of the rock, the closeness of the edge, the power of the wind. She reassures me, says all the right things, but her voice is thin and uncertain, distracted. "Are you busy?" I ask her.

"Sorry, I'm—kind of—upset. I had a fight with Wendy last night." She laughs uneasily. "It was so ridiculous."

"What about?"

"Honestly? It was like—whatever I said all night bothered her. She wasn't happy with anything. But the actual fight was about whether a dessert fork goes on the left side of the plate or at the top of the plate. My cousin's caterer had put the forks on the left, and—well, it doesn't matter."

"Ohhh."

"I know, right? It's insane. I wish I knew what's wrong with her lately."

"Have you asked her?"

"Of course! She keeps saying there's nothing wrong, that she just has a lot of homework and a lot of commitments."

"I'm sure it'll blow over. Maybe she had a headache or a test coming up, or something." I can't really understand why Sylvie is worried. Everything has a way of working out for her; everyone loves her. She's been with Wendy for more than six months, and they're perfect together. Unlike some people I could name, Wendy did not avoid her for two days after their first kiss, did not leap gratefully on a "let's be friends instead" message. It's going to take a lot more than dessert forks to tear them apart. "It'll work out."

Sylvie sighs. "I hope so."

"So listen, do you think I'll get over this panic attack or whatever it was?" I ask, and we talk about that for a few more minutes before hanging up.

My mind is not on colleges, but at dinner Mom reminds me she's waiting for my list of the ones I want to visit this year.

"I've started looking," I say. "But I don't have a list yet."

"What's taking so long?"

"Relax, Mom, we have time." I wish Dad were here—he might act as a buffer between us, get her to ease up a little. Remind her that it's only September of my junior year. But he's working late, tending the grid again.

She clanks the serving spoon into the dish of macaroni and cheese. "You need to get on this, Maggie. There are travel arrangements to make, and time off isn't always easy for me to get, with my work schedule."

"I know."

"Maybe you should make a table or a database, with all the pros and cons of the different schools." That is undoubtedly what she would do. Her eyes glow like Christmas lights when she says the word *database*.

I can't tell her I've been distracted by Nick and the whole kissing fiasco, or by watching Raleigh for signs that she might threaten me. As much as Mom wants me to be involved in social life at school, she's always said that grades come first. She would tell me to keep my brain where it belongs.

"Aren't you looking forward to it?" she says. "This is the most exciting time of your life. So many new changes coming. So many opportunities." She gazes at the cabinets as if they're screens showing reruns of her own years at nursing school.

I've heard all about those days: how she would go to classes, work for a plumbing business in the afternoons, and study at night. When she started doing shifts at the hospital, she was often on her feet for twenty-four hours or more. "It felt like the bones were coming right through the bottoms of my feet," she's told me. She lived in a dorm, surviving on ramen noodles and tuna, hanging her wet clothes on a line strung across the room instead of paying to use the dryers in the laundry room. "Every time I crossed the room, I'd end up slapping myself in the head with a soggy bra or towel," she's said, laughing.

None of that sounds like fun to me, but she loves to reminisce. Maybe she's just proud of having survived it. When she gets together with friends from nursing school, their laughter fills the house. "Remember how old McLaughlin always tried to mess us up during the practical exams?" "And how Lily passed out the first time she had to give an injection?" "Remember when Katie singed off her eyebrows in organic chemistry?" Taking care of sick people, saving lives, and backing up new doctors in training has made them unshakable. They all have that capable-warrior look, as if they could handle the apocalypse with nothing more than a screwdriver, some duct tape, and a plastic bag or two.

"I struggled so much to pay for nursing school," Mom says now, over the macaroni. "I want you to have an easier ride, if we can manage it. Scholarships, maybe, instead of so many loans."

"I'm keeping my grades up."

"I know, but Phoebe and I were talking to some of the other nurses today. They say good grades aren't enough for colleges anymore. You need activities, too."

"I did that internship last summer. I hike, I play the piano—"

"I mean organized activities. Clubs and sports teams. Phoebe and I notice that you and Nick don't belong to those kinds of groups."

I imagine Nick's mom must be having this same conversation with him right now. Except that Nick has the basketball team. And student council, too. Nick got elected as his home-room rep last year because he was absent on the day they voted, and he got reelected this year because of inertia. Maybe at other schools the council matters, maybe the kids are into it and they do important things, but at our school the adminis-tration squashed the life out of the students ages ago, and the council has no power. All it means is that once a month Nick has to eat lunch in the council meeting. According to him, they argue over such fascinating issues as whether to hold *two* School Spirit Days a year, as they always have, or take the bold move of upping that to *three*.

Also, he says they sometimes fight over nuances in Robert's Rules of Order.

"Six hours of school and three hours of homework are enough," I say. "My days are too long already." And that's true, but it's not even the biggest reason I've never joined a club. Clubs and teams are like the worst parts of school, magnified: a place where people don't even have to *pretend* to accept you, the way they have to pretend in class. Clubs mean spending more time around people like Raleigh and Adriana, who join everything in sight.

Mom spears a piece of broccoli. She brings it toward her mouth but then holds it there, as if it's a beacon lighting my way on the path toward higher education. "Well, there must be some activities at school you could join. What about the school newspaper?"

"We don't have a newspaper."

"No newspaper? I *am* getting old. What do you have?"

"There are a bunch of sports, none of which I'm good at. There's a marching band, which doesn't use a piano. A chorus, but I don't sing. Student council, but everyone was elected the first week of school."

"I was in the drama club," she says. "That was always fun. By the time I was a senior, I even had a couple of leading roles."

Sometimes I wonder if I was switched at birth in the hospital. How can my mom and I be related, but so different? "When I give an oral report in history class, the teacher complains that I don't project past the second row," I say. "I doubt I'm meant for the stage."

She takes a slice of tomato. "Well, Maggie, you need to find something. I've always thought you should have more of a social life, and colleges won't consider you if you're not well-rounded."

I think of woodworking, and the trails, and my piano music. My life is "well-rounded," even if it doesn't fit into neat little college-application slots. Nick and I get so much out of hiking, even though it isn't a formal activity, and he gets nothing out of student council, which is. I don't want to join things just so I can list them on an application.

I know how expensive college is. And I love that my mom wants to help me get there, no matter what.

But . . . if only the school had a club that truly meant something to me.

What would that be, though? A mushroom identification

club? Even if I could manage to start one myself, I doubt anyone else would join, or that it would put me on Harvard's must-
have list.

"There must be something for you," Mom says.

I shrug.

"Maggie, you can't live inside a shell for the rest of your
life. You can't rely on other people to do all the work in social
situations. You have to approach them. Join in. Take some
initiative."

I go numb for a second, and then it's as if someone has poured
hornets through a hole in the top of my head. They swarm
and sting, filling my blood, replacing my bones. Because what I
hear is, *If you don't fit in, Maggie, it's your own fault for being so . . .*

So shy? So cautious? So different? So clueless? For being so
me?

I'm shocked to find a block of compressed tears choking
me. Old, concentrated tears, left over from junior high. I drop
my fork and push away from the table, wooden-limbed, hot
and cold.

I don't cry. I go up to my room and struggle through homework. I pore over the mushroom guide, reading about chante-
relles, which are supposed to be delicious and fragrant, apricot-
scented.

Mom knocks on my door. "Can I come in?"

"I guess."

She opens the door, walks in, and sits on the bed beside me. I can't meet her eyes.

"You seemed upset by our talk earlier. Did I say something wrong? I was only trying to help."

"Well, I guess you can't help it if I'm a loser—but neither can I."

"Maggie, you're not a loser. And that isn't what I meant."

"If you don't think I'm a loser, why are you always trying to improve me?"

"We all have things we can improve. That's why I take those extra certification classes. And . . . I've been trying to lose ten pounds for ten years now." She laughs uncomfortably and extends her hand, though not quite daring to touch me. "I believe we can always make ourselves better. That doesn't mean I see any of us as losers."

"What if I don't want to be friends with a million people, the way Sylvie is?" I say. "What if I like being quiet and having a lot of time alone?"

"That's fine, but you have too much time alone." She pauses. "Maggie, I love you and I know you're a smart, talented, wonderful girl. I just wish you would give more people a chance to discover that." She kisses my forehead and gets up. "Okay?"

"Mm," I answer. And even though she has said the supposedly right things, a sourness lingers at the back of my throat. I can't escape the feeling that I don't measure up, that I never will.

"Your dad's home now. We're going to watch *Casablanca*. Want to join us?"

It's one of their favorites: doomed romance, and people who are way more heroic than I am. It's the last thing I can stand to see right now. "No, thanks," I say. "I have homework."

As soon as she's out of the room, I sigh. The worst part of this is that I know she's right—at least about beefing up my applications. Some of the teachers at school have said the same thing, and the admissions forms I've seen all ask about activities.

Ugh.

What can I do about it? Every activity I can think of, everything we mentioned at the dinner table, has a strike against it, a reason it's not for me.

It's not fair that this same old social stuff might keep me out of college. Why can't college just be about your studies?

Maybe there's something I've missed. I should double-check the school clubs, make sure they haven't magically added a mushroom club or something else that's perfect for me when I wasn't looking.

I go to the school website and scroll through the list of activities, but nothing's new.

Why isn't there a hiking club or something like that?

That gives me an idea. I look up some of the environmental groups in the area, to see what options they have for students. One has a special program called "Hands-on Conservation." They do park cleanups and trail maintenance, that kind of thing, all outdoors. Now this is the kind of group I could join.

I fill out the online application. If they accept me, I'll need Mom's permission, but after tonight's talk she can hardly say no.

I hit SEND with a shaking finger, realizing that if this group doesn't want me, it'll hurt much worse than rejection by Raleigh and her crowd. I never pretended to have much in common with Raleigh, but this is a club where I *should* fit right in.

I only hope that my failure on Crystal isn't a sign that the woods are rejecting me now, too. Because if I don't belong there anymore, either, where do I belong?

seventeen

On Monday I'm in the girls' room at school, wrestling with the toilet paper that they jam into the holder so tightly you can only tear off tiny shreds at a time, when a girl out at the sinks says, "So, you and Nick Cleary, huh?"

I peek through the crack around the edges of the stall door. Vanessa Webb leans toward the mirror, sliding lip balm across her mouth. Janie Fletcher stands beside her, fingering the ends of her own hair.

"I can't believe how people talk at this school," Vanessa says. "Anything happens, and the whole world knows in a day."

"It's true, then?"

"Depends on what you heard." Vanessa smiles at her reflection.

"What *should* I have heard?"

Vanessa laughs. "He came over yesterday."

I spent my Sunday trying new pieces on the piano, researching colleges, and arguing with my mother about whether my favorite pair of jeans was comfortably broken in (my opinion) or ready for the trash can (hers). After that, we fought about the fact that the last time I'd done the laundry, I had ruined her clean-towel-rotation system.

I didn't hear from Nick all day, but I had no idea he was at Vanessa's. I knew, from their eye-lock at the party, from his taking pictures on the mountain for her, that he was interested in her. But I never guessed he would act on it so quickly.

"Aaaand?" Janie asks.

"We talked. You know."

"I *don't* know. That's why I'm asking." Janie lets go of her hair, stands back from the mirror, and tugs at her shirt. "Did he kiss you?"

"Why, Jane Fletcher, I'm shocked that you would ask such a question." Vanessa's tone is playful, mock-offended, her lips pursed, her eyes still laughing. "What kind of girl do you think I am?"

Janie bumps her, hip to hip. "Don't tell me he didn't even try!"

"I won't tell you *that*. . . ."

I may puke. Good thing there's a toilet so close by.

"I thought he was going out with that girl Maggie, what's her last name . . ."

"He says he isn't. And she told me the same thing. They're just friends."

"So, is he any good?"

Vanessa smiles again, her eyes on the mirror. She tucks away the tube of lip balm. "Better than good."

"Oh, now you *have* to tell me!"

"Well—I swear he reads my mind or something." Vanessa pauses. "Like, he knows when to slow down and when to get more intense. It's—good, that's all." She fluffs her hair. "He doesn't act like he's God's gift to girls, the way Marcus did."

Janie snorts. "Marcus. I don't know why you ever went out with him." She turns sideways and smoothes her shirt over her stomach. "So, about Nick: I want the whole story. Details. Where were you, and who started it? And did he try to shove his tongue down your throat right away, or did he wait, like a gentleman?"

They both burst out laughing at the word *gentleman*. In the stall, I clamp my lips together queasily, thinking, *Please, no details.*

"All right, Miss Gotta-Know-Everything. We were talking in the living room, and my parents were in the kitchen where they could eavesdrop. James wasn't home, and I asked Nick if he wanted to see James's aquariums. I'd already shown him the aquariums at the party, so I knew if he said yes, that meant he wanted to be alone with me."

"And he said yes."

"We went into James's room and I closed the door, and we stared at each other, and he kept looking at my mouth but not making a move. So I said, 'The least you can do is kiss me, after I went to all this trouble to get us some privacy.' He laughed and then he leaned in and did it. He said, 'I just wanted to be sure you wanted to.'"

"Yeah, definitely not like Marcus," Janie says. "You're lucky your brother is a tropical-fish freak. Any time you want to get out of the room, all you have to do is say, 'Let's go look at the aquariums!' I only wish my brother was that useful."

They laugh again, and Vanessa says, "Let's go. I want to see if we can catch Emily before class."

I stay in the stall after they leave, running Vanessa's words through my mind on an endless loop: *Better than good. Better than good.*

So Nick has been kissing Vanessa. I think of the lip balm rolling over her mouth. Nick's mouth there, touching hers. Her brother's aquariums bubbling away in the background. The watery blue light washing over them, and Nick kissing her the way he kissed me.

I squeeze my eyes shut and lean my forehead against the metal door.

I'm about to leave the stall when Raleigh Barringer comes into the girls' room, her heels clicking on the tile floor. I hold my breath, my hand still on the latch, praying she won't know I'm here. She goes into another stall and bangs the door shut, and I wait.

I'm not moving until she's gone. I even consider pulling my feet up, so she can't tell I'm here.

Since junior high, I've done my best never to be in the girls' room with her. She and Lissa Carpenter once trapped me in a stall.

"You can't come out," Lissa giggled that day, "until you admit you wash your hair in the toilet."

"Everyone knows it," Raleigh said. "I mean, if you ever wash it at all!"

Lissa laughed so hard she could barely speak. "Did you think we couldn't tell?"

I huddled in my stall. So many times, I was defenseless because they would pick on ways in which I knew I wasn't perfect, even though they exaggerated. I washed my hair every day, but it was thin and staticky, and tended to tangle. I'd tried conditioner, but that made it flat and greasy looking. Still, no matter what else was wrong with my hair, at least it was clean.

Raleigh held her phone up over the stall door. Those doors were never high enough; tall girls could peek over them if they tiptoed. "I'll record it," she said. "Just say it, and then you can come out."

"No," I said.

She hammered on the door. "Say it! Everyone knows it's true, anyway."

"No."

"If you don't say it, you can never come out. You'll die in there."

I sat on the toilet seat with my pants pulled up. I would out-wait them. They had to get bored after a while, didn't they?

Except Raleigh never got bored when it came to tormenting me.

They waited, banging on the door and screaming at me from time to time. I read the graffiti scratched into the wall: *I luv Brian. Maggie Camden sucks. JV + MT. Ashlee + Ed 4eva!!!* I wished there was something interesting written there. Evidently, nobody had ever foreseen the need for reading material in case of imprisonment.

Sometimes the outer door creaked when other girls came into the restroom. The footsteps always started out bold and quick, then paused, and I knew that was when they spotted Raleigh and Lissa. Then the steps would patter quietly back out the door.

I didn't call for help. Who would help me? Everyone knew better than to mess with Raleigh.

I didn't break until the bell rang at the end of lunch. I could not stand to read *Maggie Camden sucks* or *Ashlee + Ed 4eva!!!* one more time. I was worried about missing my afternoon classes. And I knew that nobody was coming to save me.

So I closed my eyes and said it. "I wash my hair in the toilet."

"What? Wait, let me get it on my phone. And louder!" Raleigh barked.

I said it again. Raleigh and Lissa howled. They played the recording, laughed until they collapsed, and played it again. And again. And again. I had to listen to myself saying those words, over and over. My voice in the recording was flat and forced, the words an obvious lie, but I knew that wouldn't matter to anyone who heard it. People believed what they wanted, not what was true.

As I knew they would, Raleigh and Lissa sent the recording around to phones throughout the school. Kids laughed over it for weeks. Even after the joke faded, someone would always bring it up again, a single jab whenever it was on the verge of being forgotten. "Maggie, what took you so long in the bathroom?" "Phew, it stinks in here. Maggie, did you just wash your hair?" "Hey, Maggie, did you discover shampoo yet?"

Now, out at the sinks, Raleigh flips her hair over her shoulder and washes her hands. I've been in this stall for a hundred years, first waiting out Vanessa, and now her.

How many times can a person rinse her hands or pluck at a stray hair? Isn't she *ever* going to leave?

At last, she stalks toward the door. For a moment, rage flashes over me. I itch to run out and knock her into one of the stalls, lock her in, make her beg to get out. See how *she* likes it.

I don't know where it comes from. I haven't felt it in years. It flares and dies, leaving me shaking.

Nick sits alone at our lunch table, scrolling through his messages. "Isn't Vanessa joining us today?" I ask.

He glances up from his phone. "I don't know."

I don't know. My stomach hardens into a block of ice. He

didn't say, "Why would Vanessa join us?" He didn't say, "What are you talking about?" She actually might sit with us.

"By the way, I can't eat with you tomorrow," he says. "Student council meeting."

"That should be exciting." I pretend to yawn. Yet I can't stop digging at the Vanessa thing. "But listen, you're the talk of the girls' room. Your kissing technique, and so forth."

He frowns and clicks off his phone. "What?"

"Vanessa—critiquing your tongue action—girls' room—fourth period."

He stares at me but doesn't bite at the bait, doesn't ask for details. His eyes stay on me until I almost want to squirm, even though I don't do that anymore. By eighth grade, I learned never to squirm on the outside, no matter what's going on inside me.

"What's your problem, Maggie?"

"I thought you'd be dying to hear the gossip." I bite into a carrot stick, trying to be casual.

"I don't care what people say."

"Not even Vanessa? You don't want to hear how she rates you?"

"If I want to know what Vanessa thinks, I'll ask her."

"So you admit you gave her something to talk about."

"*Admit?* What am I, under arrest?" He shuffles his long legs beneath the table. They stretch under the seat next to me. "I went to Vanessa's house yesterday. Since you're so interested. If you want to ask me about it, Maggie, just ask—what do you want to know?"

The carrot is like a wooden twig in my mouth. My face burns. I shake my head.

Bio lab with Raleigh's best friend is not the way I want to finish off the day, but I've been getting used to Adriana. The sound of her voice no longer slices into my nerves quite as much as it did before. Although whenever someone makes a joke in class, her sudden cackle causes me to jump.

Today Thornhart has us build double helices out of blocks and pegs. When our DNA models are built, Thornhart comes by to pull things out and shift them around, and then we have to repair them. "Enzymes do this work in the real world," he says. Then we make RNA strands from our model DNA, and from DNA that's been mutated by our teacher's hands. We unwind our models and re-create the missing strands from the existing strands.

"I guess this does help you remember how everything works," Adriana says as we take apart our models at the end of class. "When you have to put it all together with your own hands, it sticks in your mind."

"Yeah," I say, tearing apart my simulated frame-shift muta-tion. For a minute, the whole room takes on a strangeness: the double helices mimicking what's going on in my cells this very minute, which I would never even know about if it weren't for bio class. It's like a glimpse of something miraculous, mysteri-ous, important: a piece of the blueprints for life itself.

Adriana says, "Did you ever look at your hand and think: 'Wow, there are all these cells dividing right now'? I mean, do you ever think how this stuff we're reading about is happening in our bodies, not just in the textbook?"

I stare at Adriana, unable to believe she has channeled my thoughts. When I don't say anything, she flushes and turns away, dumping her blocks and pegs into the storage box.

Ethan Crannick waits at the door. His eyes are blank, gliding past me to settle on Adriana. Her voice gets even higher than usual, more animated, as she takes his hand. I slip away, putting distance between them and me. I can't forget that Adriana is still Adriana. She and Raleigh used to trick me sometimes, tempt me to think the punishment might be over with. They would back off for a while, maybe even hold open a door for me or say something nice. Which made it all the more vicious when they started up again, never letting me have more than a day or two of rest.

Adriana and I may get along all right while we're sitting at a lab bench, but it would be stupid to let down my guard.

eighteen

Vanessa is eating lunch with Nick and me.

It had to happen sooner or later. In the three days since I overheard her describe Nick's kisses, I've seen her with him in the halls. Her name has flashed across his cell-phone screen.

Last weekend wasn't a one-time thing. She really is his girlfriend.

She freshens her lip gloss, and the fluorescent cafeteria light bounces off it. I tried wearing lip gloss back in eighth grade, but I hated the way it felt on my mouth, the stickiness of it. Does Nick enjoy kissing lip gloss, I wonder? Does any guy? Or maybe some do and some don't?

"*Bonjour,* Marguerite," Vanessa says through shining lips.

"*Bonjour.*" I sigh.

"Are you going to join the French club? I'm president this year."

"French club? Oh—no—I don't think so."

"I hear you and Nick have been trying to climb Crystal Mountain."

"That's right." Has he told her about my panic attack? If he has, she doesn't bring it up.

Nick plucks a French fry off Vanessa's plate. I hate that, the casualness of it. The intimacy of his reaching over to her tray without asking, and the way she smiles and welcomes it. Especially since Nick has always been almost as closed off as I am, almost as shy, almost as slow to trust people. He mostly interacts with people by passing them a basketball. How can he be so relaxed with her?

It makes me feel so *extra*. Even though they're including me in the conversation. The heat between them is impossible to ignore. Next thing you know, they'll be heading up the home-coming committee and hosting joint beach parties, and doing whatever else class-couple types do.

I choke down my sandwich and tell myself not to be ridiculous. I know Nick, and he's not about to fall into lockstep with Vanessa, exchanging cutesy nicknames, matching his clothes to hers.

And he'll still be my hiking partner. Even if we can't (okay, if I can't) tackle the Cinnamon Range, we'll still do the Cannon Lake and Hemlock Brook hikes, visit the county parks and wildlife preserves, the way we always have. We'll still go to the woods.

I think.

*   *   *

Vanessa doesn't ride home with us, maybe because she has her own car and lives in the opposite direction. Luis cranks up the music on the ride to his place, saying, "Listen to that guitar. Just *listen* to that!"

"Why?" Nick says. "Is it going to reveal a secret code?"

Luis grimaces at him. "You should hear these guys in concert! It'll change your life." In desperation, he turns to me. "Maggie, you know music. Isn't that guitar incredible?"

"Piano's my instrument."

Luis rolls his eyes toward the car roof, groaning. But the truth is that I probably could appreciate the guitar more if I weren't thinking so much about Vanessa, still feeling her presence at Nick's side.

When we pull up at Luis's and he's getting out of the car, Nick stops him by saying, "Hey, Morales."

"What?"

Nick gazes at him so seriously I start to wonder what's wrong. Apparently, Luis does, too; his face takes on a waiting, even fearful, look.

"I wanted to let you know," Nick says. "After hearing the rest of that song on the way over here . . . *my life is changed.*"

Luis swats him, but they're both laughing as Luis climbs out of the car. "Hell, Cleary, I try to give your sad little life some meaning, and this is what I get."

"Well, thanks for trying," Nick says. Luis trudges up the driveway, shaking his head.

I get in the front, as usual. Maybe it would make sense for

me to ride in the front the whole time, but we've always done it this way, with me switching seats halfway through the ride. I don't mind. Luis has more of a front-seat personality than I do.

As Nick backs out of the driveway, I ask him, "Should I come over?"

"Better not. I've got a ton of homework to get through if I want to go out tonight."

"Out—with Vanessa?"

"Uh-huh."

I can't stop thinking of them together, Nick kissing her shiny mouth.

The thing is, it's none of my business anymore.

Besides, there's nothing wrong with Vanessa. It's not like Nick is hooking up with Raleigh Barringer. He deserves some happiness, right? Good for him.

I try to change my mental channel, but the same image keeps playing.

"What do you guys talk about, anyway?" I ask. "I know she's not into hiking. Or basketball."

"Well, last night we talked about how she wants to work in Africa."

"Africa?"

"Yeah—that's why she's taking French. She wants to work for a relief organization."

"She does? Wow. I didn't know that."

"Now you do."

"Yes . . ." I try to imagine Vanessa doing relief work in Africa.

I've never seen her with a spot on her shirt or a wrinkle in her pants. Her nails are never even chipped.

"And sometimes we talk about movies," Nick continues.

"Oh."

"Should I record our next conversation for you?"

"Nick!" I force a casual tone. "Yeah, do that. Might as well get a video clip, too."

He laughs.

"When's our next hike?" I ask.

"I haven't thought about it. Why, when do you want to go?"

"This weekend?"

"I can't—it's my weekend to see my father." He says "see my father" in the same tone of voice most people would use to say "get a tetanus shot."

"Oh."

"I'd rather hike with you, Maggie, believe me," he says while I'm gathering my stuff. "Dad never knows what to do with me."

I adopt an infomercial-announcer voice. "But you're a multi-purpose son, handy for a wide variety of household activities."

"Ha-ha. He thinks I'm useless."

"Why do you say that?"

"His whole life is proteins. What do I know about proteins? Once he told me I couldn't tell an amino terminus from a carboxy terminus. I'm guessing that's a great insult among biochemists." He glances at his pile of homework in the backseat. "I'll probably bring *Julius Caesar* with me. I have to finish reading it sometime."

"Yeah, I can see you and your dad sitting around reading Shakespeare. Maybe you can act out the parts."

"Not unless I get to be Brutus."

"Nick, I'm sensing a little hostility toward your father."

"Only a little?" Before I can answer, he says, "I should get going. I'll call you later." And I open the car door.

On Friday night, while Nick is with his dad and Sylvie's with Wendy, I go to the local library to work on my history paper. I'm outlining an essay about unions and the labor movement when Darci Esposito passes my table with Raleigh Barringer at her heels.

My blood freezes in my veins. The girls don't seem to see me, but head for the reference room at the back of the library. "Find your glasses and then let's *go*," Raleigh tells Darci. "How'd you manage to leave them here in the first place? Didn't you notice that you couldn't see?"

Every time I think I've gotten used to Raleigh being back in town, one glimpse sends me into fight-or-flight mode. I start typing again, but enough adrenaline floods my system to power the town for a week. Dad should hook me up to the grid. My fingers tremble on the keyboard as the junior high memories crowd my brain.

Messages would sweep through the neighborhood: **Everyone kick Maggie tomorrow. Maggie is the ugliest girl in seventh grade. Tomorrow is trip Maggie day.** I knew about them because Virginia Loughlin, a pale, skinny girl who sat behind me in history, forwarded them to me. She was on the fringes herself, escaping their wrath only because I was the main target. **I'm so sorry . . .** she would text me when she sent on the messages. **I just want you to be prepared. . . . I'm sorry I can't talk to you at school because they would get me, too. . . .**

I sit motionless as Darci and Raleigh come out of the reference room and pass me again. I might be a statue: *Girl Doing Homework.* They ignore me and I exhale, but my fingers still have trouble finding the right keys.

What if I had stuck out my foot when Raleigh passed my table? I could pretend it was an accident. Or I could look at her as she lay on the floor and say, "It must be Trip Raleigh Day."

With my luck, she'd step right over my foot. Or *on* it, crushing my toes.

I don't have the nerve to trip her, anyway.

My phone vibrates in the quiet library. I check it and find a message from Nick: **Help! I'm stuck with a mad scientist.**

I type back: **Is this mad scientist by any chance related to you?**

He replies: **You guessed it.**

Where are you?

Restaurant. Really on the sidewalk outside—supposed to be in the men's room. He spent the last hour telling me what an idiot I am. I'm thinking of walking home.

He'd come after you.

True. The only way I can get through this weekend is to think about next weekend. I need a hike.

So do I.

Crystal?

Ha-ha.

I'm serious. Get right back on the horse, and all that.

I stare at my phone. I know I need to go back. The hiking trails are the one place I've felt like my real self, the one place I've belonged, and I can't accept the defeat on Crystal. Once you give fear a toehold, it pushes for more. The thought of not going back—of letting my cringing failure stand forever—starts to creep under my skin. I don't want to feel limited on the trails. Inadequate, the way I feel in the school halls.

But I had hoped to have a little more breathing room before trying again; I want to prepare. It's only been a week. I type: What, you have mountain fever now?

I need to get away from here and forget about everything else.

Why should he want to forget about "everything?" What about Vanessa?

I don't ask. I'm actually glad that he still wants to hike, that he won't spend all his free time glued to her side. If only I felt more secure about tackling Crystal.

I answer: **I don't know if I can do it.**

Think about it, his message says. **While I try to survive this weekend.**

You'll survive. Feel free to text the Maggie Lifeline anytime.

Thanks, lifeline.

Back at home, I call Sylvie. "You busy?"

"Just trying to turn an old tennis racket into a banjo for my brother's school talent show," she says. "I was waiting for Wendy to call, but now I don't think she's going to."

"How is your brother going to strum a tennis racket?"

"He doesn't really have to play music. Just sing. 'Oh! Susanna.' Except he doesn't sing it so much as yell it. What are you up to?"

"Having a crisis. You know that mountain where I had a panic attack? Nick wants to go back."

"Well, he can go back. You don't have to."

That's true, of course. But the thought of Nick going while I stay home staring at my idle boots and backpack is too much.

Would he really go back alone? Or even with Vanessa?

Maybe not with Vanessa. Nick has said that Crystal isn't for beginners, and he's right. "I want to go," I tell Sylvie. "I'm just scared. But I want to prove I can do it."

"Well, maybe you should. The first time I had to give a speech in class, when I was eight, I ran and hid behind the teacher's desk. But after that, it got easier."

I can't imagine Sylvie hiding, Sylvie scared. Is she making up that story so I'll feel better?

"Do you think I can do it?" I ask, fishing for a pep talk.

"Sure, why not? You climbed that other mountain, right?"

"But that was easier."

"If I can make a banjo out of a tennis racket, which I've never done before, you can hike a trail, which you *have* done before." Her tone is light, joking, but I would swear there's an edge of impatience to it. Or maybe she's just tired.

I stop myself from begging for more reassurance, more guarantees. Instead, I tell her, "You've inspired me."

"Good."

"Yes, I now believe I can make a fake banjo."

She laughs, the edge dissolving from her voice.

After I hang up with her, I flip through my mushroom book, losing myself in the names. Saffron parasol, poison powder puff, velvet foot. Tawny milkcap, orange peel, gem-studded puffball. Honeycomb morel, mica cap, destroying angel.

Maybe most people wouldn't see this as a fun Friday night, but I've never found a book as fascinating as my mushroom book. There's so much power here: food or poison, life or death. In my guide, they're mixed together, the edible ones and the ones that kill. On the trail I never touch a mushroom, even if I think it's safe.

You never know.

I reread the guide to the Crystal hike, picturing myself

tackling it again. I try to mentally shepherd myself past the place where I froze last time: the ledges where the exposure, the sheer sense of height, made me dizzy. The spot where my legs locked, where every drop of confidence drained out the bottoms of my feet.

I close my eyes and picture it, trying sports psychology–style mental cheerleading. *I am brave! I am strong! I can climb this mountain!* All this does is make me want to giggle. I guess seeing three minutes of a sports psychologist interview on TV doesn't make me an expert.

But nervous as I am, I don't want to back away from this.

Over the weekend, I talk Nick off the proverbial ledge four more times, which is average for a weekend with his father. To keep his spirits up, I remind him of Crystal, even though I tell him I need more time before going back to the Cinnamon Range. But I quote the trail guide to him: "'The sheer cliffs and steep climbs of the Crystal Mountain trail make it unsuitable for beginners, but strong hikers should have no serious trouble.'" Which I realize would not cheer up anyone else on the planet, but that's Nick.

But during the school week, it's as if none of that happened, as if he never called the Maggie Lifeline. I rarely see Nick alone. On Monday, he doesn't even show up at our lunch table. I guess he's with Vanessa, because I don't see her, either.

I'm not sure which is harder: seeing him with Vanessa, or not seeing them at all and wondering where they've slipped off to. In French class, I study Vanessa's dreamy smile for any signs that she's been with Nick at lunch. Talking with him. Making out with him. Or—

If Nick lost his virginity, he would tell me, wouldn't he? I can't imagine him not telling me something that big.

On the other hand, I can't imagine him announcing it, either.

But they've only been together for a couple of weeks. Surely nothing that intense is happening yet? Even if you could practically light a bonfire from the heat between them. Even if they lose all awareness of whoever else is around them when they're together.

On Tuesday, hoping to avoid them, I go to the library instead of the cafeteria. But it's just my luck to catch a glimpse of them in a far corner of the library: Nick's hand stroking her shoulder, their mouths meeting with an intensity that makes me dizzy, hungry, lonely, embarrassed to see it.

When Nick drives me to and from school, Luis is in the car for most of the ride. I sit in the car behind Nick, trying not to stare at the back of his head. Trying to make myself stop wanting what I want.

nineteen

This week, I go to the piano every night. The music I choose is dark and heavy as thunder: stormy pieces with plenty of *crescendo* and *fortissimo* and left-hand keys. It's the waves from a hurricane breaking on a beach, the huge curls you get when a storm is out at sea. I used to play these songs a lot in junior high. Lately, I've been hungry for the piano again, playing more than ever.

Mom hovers, trying to lift me out of my "moodiness." She has just gone through a closet-cleaning frenzy, and I shoot down her suggestion that I sort through the boxes of elementary-school projects, leaf collections, and seashells under my bed.

I do give her my college list. She has me go back and reorganize it geographically, cross-referencing it by how much I want to attend each school, but it's finally finished. I've picked ten schools all over the Northeast. It's still hard for me to believe that I will finish high school someday, that I won't be stuck here forever. It's a fantasy, a fairy tale: something I've dreamed of without ever expecting it to come true. I have another half of high school to get through.

And even then . . . what if I don't belong at college, either? I've been assuming it will be better than high school, but what if I'm wrong? This time I'll probably get away from Raleigh for good, but what if there are Raleigh Barringers everywhere?

Dad asks me to sand the bench he made for Grandma. The sanding burns off my nervous energy; I do it until my arms ache. When Dad checks my work and runs his fingers over the wood, he doesn't have to tell me it's a good job. Even before he smiles, I know. And it's a relief to have done something right this week, to have helped make something real and solid and worthwhile.

On Wednesday, again, Nick and Vanessa don't come to lunch. Sitting by myself, with a ring of empty seats around me that implies I might be carrying polio, I pull out my phone and text Sylvie. **Where are you?**

Yearbook committee. You?

Alone in the caf, where else? Nick is never around anymore. He's always busy.

Tell me about it. Wendy's busy all the time, too.

I don't think this is the same kind of busy.

I hope not!!

I'm sure you have nothing to worry about. Wendy has a lot to do in college, right?

When she doesn't answer, I send: **Are you there?** a couple of times.

Sorry. We had to take a vote here. What color cover to put on the yearbook.

Well, don't keep me in suspense!

Blue. A pause, then: **I should go now. They expect me to participate.**

At the end of lunch, Sylvie and I cross paths in the girls' room. I check for feet beneath the stall doors, and she asks, "Why do you always do that?"

"Checking for ambushes," I say without thinking.

"'Ambushes?!'" she says with an uneasy laugh, unsure if I'm joking.

I hesitate. "It's a leftover habit from junior high."

That's all I say, and she doesn't ask for more. I suppose I've just told her all she ever needs to know about my junior high experience.

I walk into bio lab to find Raleigh at my bench, arguing with Adriana. I creep toward Raleigh as if she's a tarantula, but she doesn't even see me. She's blocking the way to my seat. I hang back, waiting.

"Ethan's such a jerk," Raleigh says. "I don't know why you ever liked him."

"But I did like him," Adriana says.

"I told you he was trouble."

"You have no right to tell me who to like."

"Oh, honestly. You're better off without him."

"Will you stop saying that?"

Raleigh sighs impatiently. "I'm only trying to help you move on. Believe me, he's not worth all this drama. He's an idiot. He wouldn't even have made it to high school without Matt giving him the answers."

Adriana's mouth tightens. "You're one to talk about giving answers!"

Raleigh recoils. Fascinated, because I've never seen her caught off guard, I inch closer.

"Don't even *think* about going there," she says in a voice so venomous, so much a part of seventh and eighth grades, that for one confused minute I'm back in junior high. She snaps, "And pull yourself together. You don't want to cry in the middle of bio lab." With that, she marches out of the room.

I take my place as the bell rings, not knowing what to say to Adriana, who stares at the benchtop. Thornhart has barely started the lecture when Adriana claps her hand over her face and runs out of the room.

Everyone stares at her empty seat, at the door. Thornhart stands with his hand in the air, still pointing at a diagram of animal-kingdom classifications. "Maggie," he says at last, "why don't you check on your partner and see if she's okay? Walk her to the nurse if that's what she needs."

I find Adriana in the girls' room, sobbing over one of the sinks. I do a quick check under the stall doors before coming to stand beside her. "What do you want?" she chokes out.

"Thornhart sent me to check on you. He thinks you're sick."

"Well, he can go on thinking it."

Tears and makeup drip down her puffy red face. I have never seen Adriana look less than perfect, and here she is with her face melting. I would've given anything to see this in junior high. I would've given anything to believe that the people who tormented me had bad moments, that they ever hurt. But now I'm only sorry for her.

"For what it's worth," I say, "I thought Raleigh was being pretty unfair to you."

"She can be such a bitch sometimes," Adriana blubbers. She runs a paper towel under the faucet and presses it to her face.

No argument there, I think, but I don't say it. I expect Adriana to make up with Raleigh, and I don't want to say anything that can be used against me.

Adriana goes on. "She had a hell of a nerve, saying that about Ethan getting answers from Matt. When *she* nearly got kicked out of West End for doing Scott Brewer's homework."

"What?"

Adriana mops off her face. "Oh yeah," she says, her voice still fierce. "At the end of eighth grade, she wrote about four English papers for Scott. They nearly got expelled. And the worst of it was, she thought he was in love with her, but once she couldn't do his homework anymore, he acted like he didn't even know her name."

I vaguely remember Scott Brewer—a boy with a bland, pretty

face and a self-satisfied smirk. Much like Raleigh's own smirk, in fact. It's hard for me to imagine Raleigh doing extra work for so much risk and so little in return. "Why did she do it?"

I hand Adriana another paper towel. She wets it and wrings it out, keeping her eyes on the sink. "She really liked him. It's the closest she ever came to having a boyfriend. He was using her, but she never saw it until the end, when her parents got called into school."

It hasn't hit me until now, but I've never seen Raleigh with a boy. With groups of boys, yes. I think of her joking with Luis at the basketball court, polished and self-assured. Drawing the other boys toward her, and then walking away as if they couldn't hold her interest. But—a boyfriend, a close relationship? No. Not unless she had one in Italy.

"She made a total fool out of herself," Adriana says. "Which Raleigh never does. But you should've heard her talking about Scott this and Scott that, how amazing he was, how in love with her he was. . . ." Grimacing, Adriana presses the towel to her eyes. "That's why it's so unfair for her to be a bitch about Ethan. She should know how I feel."

Adriana might as well expect sympathy from the bathroom sink she's leaning over, but I won't waste my breath telling her that. I'm far more interested in Raleigh's past, anyway.

"Why *didn't* they kick her out of school?"

"She would kill me if she knew I told you this. But— do you swear not to tell anyone?"

"Yes," I say. Though I'm not sure if I mean it. Why should

I keep any promise to Adriana, or agree to protect Raleigh?

Adriana lowers the towel, glances around the empty bathroom, and drops her voice. "Raleigh's parents almost broke up that year. Her father was involved with someone else and everything. That's why they went to Italy, so her parents could work on their marriage—which I guess they did, because they're still together. So, because Raleigh was having such a hard time at home and was leaving for Italy, anyway, they decided not to expel her. And Scott ended up transferring to Hayward so they wouldn't expel him."

So much for the "zero tolerance" policy against cheating that West End always used to brag about. Even now, more than two years later, I resent the school officials for not expelling Raleigh. God knows it would've made my life easier.

But beneath my anger is a seed of surprise that Raleigh is human.

Not that her troubles excuse what she did to me. According to Adriana, Raleigh's problems happened in eighth grade, and she started her war against me early in seventh.

"I shouldn't have said anything," Adriana says, dabbing at the mascara stains on her cheeks. "It's just—she makes me so mad sometimes."

"I know," I murmur.

"Please promise me you'll keep it to yourself. Her family doesn't need this hashed over again."

"Mm," I say, which I tell myself could be a yes or could be a no.

Raleigh, a cheater. Nearly expelled. Used and dumped by Scott Brewer—a trap I would've guessed she'd be too smart and too self-centered to fall into.

It's the first time I've ever seen any real weakness in Raleigh. And something dark and strong stirs deep inside me, an energy I've never felt before.

I know that Sylvie would tell me to pretend I've never heard all this. Not only because she doesn't know my full history with Raleigh, but because I can't imagine her encouraging revenge—against anyone, for any reason.

But . . .

Oh my God. After all Raleigh did to me. If she had known such things about me, she wouldn't have hesitated to use them. *Maggie, why did you really go to Italy? Hey, Maggie, do you wipe Scott Brewer's ass for him, too? You didn't truly believe that a guy could like you, did you?*

I once told Nick about imagining her blue faced from poisoning. But that was always unreal, a fantasy. I let my imagination run free because I never expected to have power over Raleigh anywhere but in my own mind. I never expected she would have any real vulnerability—to me, least of all.

For now, there's comfort simply in holding this information to myself. Cradling it, weighing it. Tasting every drop of its rich bittersweetness.

twenty

Hard as it is to eat lunch alone on the days when Sylvie has a club meeting, it's not much easier to eat with Nick and Vanessa.

They show up together in the cafeteria the day after I learn Raleigh's secret. Sitting across from me, they eat off each other's plates. It's like tagging along on a honeymoon, and I want to bury my head in the giant tub of cafeteria coleslaw. Instead I smile, and chew my food, and answer Vanessa's questions. Lunch lasts approximately seventy-four thousand hours.

"You should try the French club, Maggie," Vanessa says. "It's a lot of fun. We've seen a couple of French films, and next week we're going to Brasserie Claude."

"No, thanks." The last thing I want is to spend more time with Vanessa. It's not her fault, but I can't stop picturing her with Nick.

She tries another subject. "Nick says you play the piano."

"Yes."

"He says you're very good."

"No."

"Yes, you are," Nick cuts in.

"Well, my teacher said I didn't challenge myself enough."

"What kind of music do you play?" Vanessa asks.

"Classical."

She's exhausted her list of questions. I don't ask her any, so the conversation collapses, an almost-visible heap on the table between us. I probably seem rude, but they don't know how much effort it takes for me to sit with them. It's all I can do to stay put and swallow my sandwich, tiny bite by tiny bite.

Nick sends me a dark look, but he doesn't say anything until we're alone in his car later, after dropping off Luis.

"Vanessa thinks you don't like her," he says.

"It's not that I don't like her."

"Can't you be nicer to her?"

"I'm trying."

"Well, she deserves better treatment than you gave her at lunch."

Maybe she does, but—doesn't he realize this might be the *slightest* bit difficult for me? Is it so easy for him to forget we ever kissed? Sometimes I still can't believe how quickly he moved from me to her.

It's hard enough to see them together, though I can grit my teeth and get through it, as long as I can keep some distance between Vanessa and me. But if I'm going to have to become one of her best friends—if Nick wants me to go out of my way to be open, enthusiastic—that's too much to take. "It's just—weird to see you spending so much time with someone else. Especially after that day in your room when we . . ."

He skids to a stop at a red light. "What are you bringing that up for?"

"Well, you know. After what happened with us, to see you kissing another girl is—"

"Jeez, Maggie. Are you kidding me? What do you care? You acted like you wanted to wash out your mouth after I kissed you."

What is he talking about?

"You ran out of the room like your hair was on fire, and then you told me you wanted to be just friends. So fine, we're friends, but don't expect me never to be with another girl. Especially one who manages to stay in the room after I touch her."

I'm breathless, stunned by his version of events. *He thinks I'm the one who didn't want him? Is that why he didn't call me?*

I've never thought anyone would worry about being rejected by me, would even see that as possible. I assumed Nick wasn't interested because I assume no guy is interested in me, ever. Because I'm ugly old Maggie, the girl who washes her hair in the toilet.

The driver behind us honks; the light has turned. Nick's car jerks forward.

I can't believe how tangled up we've gotten. If only we'd had this conversation weeks ago. If only I'd listened to Sylvie and called him right away.

Because now there's Vanessa.

I clear my throat, searching for my voice. "Nick, I—this is complicated, but . . ."

No, forget complicated. Forget trying to fix the past, trying to compete with Vanessa.

Stick with the simplest truth.

"You've been my best friend for years. And I . . . miss you."

His face relaxes. "Yeah, I know what you mean." For a minute, I think we're okay. Until he adds: "But things can't stay the same forever."

The familiar streets stream past my window. I chew on the inside of my cheek, telling myself I will not cry.

Ordinarily, we're good at being quiet together, at talking without words. It works on the trail, where all we need to communicate is when to pause for water or check the map. But today, we might as well be on different planets. In spite of all we've said about staying friends, I can't stop feeling that we've lost something we can never get back.

"Maggie," he says, his voice warmer now. "I still—"

"Forget it," I cut in. I don't want to hear that he still likes me as a friend and will try to fit me into the spare moments of his life. I can't stand thinking about what might've happened between us if I hadn't been too scared, if I hadn't made too many wrong assumptions.

We turn onto my street. "Just—give me some room," I say. With enough space to collect myself, maybe I can keep from cracking apart right in front of him. Get used to his being with

Vanessa, never let him know how much more I wanted. Maybe I'll get to keep a scrap of dignity.

"That's what you want? Room?"

"Yes."

We stop in front of my house.

"You can have all the room you want," he says as I get out. He drives off without a good-bye.

I lie on my bed, thumbing through my mushroom guide, but in my head I'm still in the car with Nick. Maybe I haven't been fair to him, but he hasn't been fair to me, either. If the situation were reversed, would he find it so easy to watch me drool over some other guy?

I stop, staring at a page without seeing it. What if I *were* with another guy? If I'd been the first one to move on—if by some miracle I'd found someone else to move on *with*—how would I want Nick to act?

The truth is, I would want him to welcome my boyfriend.

I would want him to be happy for me.

I would not want him to sulk, or glower at my boyfriend, or act like someone had invaded his territory.

Groaning, I put down the book. I find my phone and text Sylvie. She doesn't answer.

But even without Sylvie's advice, I know what I have to do.

I text Nick. **Forget what I said. I'm happy for you and I'm going**

to be nice to Vanessa. I have no idea *how* I'll manage this, but I'm going to try. It's what a friend should do.

I expect him to text back, but he doesn't.

He calls.

"Got your message," he says.

"I meant what I said. If you really like her, then I'll—"

"Yeah, I like her. I wouldn't be with her otherwise. But—"

That word hangs in the air.

"But what?"

"Nothing. I like her. She doesn't play games, and she knows what she wants." *Unlike you,* is the unspoken message.

I gather every ounce of brightness and bravery I can scrape up. "Fine. If you like her, I like her." I still don't know how I'm going to deal with this. The thought of being around her—watching her touch him—hurts. But I'm trying. "I'll be nice to her."

"Thanks, Maggie."

When we hang up, I go downstairs and pound through some scales on the piano. My playing has been getting sloppy, and my teacher used to say that there are times you have to go back to basics. Order and precision, I tell myself as my fingers march through the monotonous octaves. Mastery. Perfection.

"For Pete's sake, Maggie, that's maddening," Mom says. I

jump, not realizing she has entered the room. "Can't you play a song instead?"

"I'm warming up my fingers."

"Well, surely they must be warmed up by now." She drops onto the couch with a groan and elevates her feet. "I was going to fix that leak in the kitchen faucet, but frankly I'm not in the mood. My legs are killing me. These young girls I work with, I tell them to wear tight stockings, anything to support their leg veins, and they laugh at me. I wish I could trade legs with them for a day." She brushes hair back from her forehead. "Why don't you play that moonlight song?"

"'The Moonlight Sonata'?"

"Yes."

It's a relief not to have to answer questions about my future, my ambitions. Maybe she's too worn-out for that right now. And I love this sonata, too.

So I play the first movement of it. There's so much *pianissimo* that it quiets me, the sound spreading over us like moonlight pouring over a lake, as Beethoven must have intended. It's dark enough for my mood, and quiet enough for my mother's. At the final soft chord, which is repeated once, we both exhale.

At lunch the next day, I carry on a real, live conversation with Vanessa. I don't promise to join her French club or help her decorate for her upcoming Halloween party, but I manage to speak to her without strangling.

"You're coming to the party, right, Maggie?" Vanessa says.

"I'm not sure. I have to ask my mom."

Nick stares at me, because he knows my mother only wishes I would go to more parties. But he doesn't call me on it.

"Don't forget, you have to wear a costume," Vanessa says. "It's more fun that way."

Ugh. Dressing up tells the world *Look at me!* when all I've ever wanted is to blend into the walls. Costumes raise my self-consciousness to near-fatal levels. The only thing worse than standing in a room full of people who barely acknowledge my right to exist—and watching the boy I like huddle with his girl-friend—would be doing all that while wearing a costume.

And then I realize that if *everyone* has to dress up . . .

"Wait. Are you telling me Nick's wearing a costume?"

"Yes."

I can't help laughing. "Good luck getting him into one." This might almost be worth going to the party for.

"Hey, it's already taken care of," Nick says.

"How?" I ask. "What are you doing, just wearing your basketball uniform?"

"Of course not," Vanessa says, but his face reddens. "Oh no, you're not!" she tells him, nudging his arm. "You have to wear a *real* costume."

"We'll see," Nick says, examining his sandwich rather than meeting her eyes.

"I'll help you if you need ideas," she says.

"Me too." I grin at him. "I have lots of ideas."

"You've been enough help already," he says with a sour smile, stealing a pickle chip from my lunch.

I walk past Raleigh's table on my way to drop off my tray. I hug her secret to myself and even dare to glance at her, when usually I would avert my eyes. I almost wish she would look up. But she doesn't notice me. Not this time.

twenty-one

A fter school, I send a few messages to Sylvie, dying to talk to her since I'm feeling farther than ever from Nick.

Sylvie, you there?

Can you talk?

Sylvie, call me when you get this.

But I don't hear from her.

It's Dad's birthday, so I take the box I've made (working in snatches of time in the afternoons when he was still out feeding the grid) and place it in the middle of the kitchen table with a red bow on it.

Mom has bought him a set of drill bits, some shirts, and tickets for the two of them to a film festival, where there probably won't be a single movie in color. Dinner is meat loaf, which I could really live without, but it's one of his favorites.

Dad holds up the box I made. "Beautiful job, Maggie." He

opens it, trying the clasp and the hinges. I'm still proud of the way those hinges open. "You're getting better and better."

"Oh, and Benny sent this," Mom says, setting down a bottle of honey-colored whiskey.

"Too bad he's not here to help me drink it," Dad says.

Dad goes out sometimes with a few guys at work, but he has one close friend—a guy to whom he'd probably give a kidney if it was necessary—and that's Benny. They grew up next door to each other, and then Benny moved two hours southeast of their hometown, and my dad moved two hours northwest. So we only see Benny every couple of years or so. Every time we see him, he's heavier, his hairline farther back, but he always has the same grin. And even though he and Dad don't see each other much nowadays, when they get together, they fall instantly into talking and joking, as if the years apart are just pauses in an ongoing conversation.

Looking at Benny's bottle, I can't help thinking about friendship. About my own birthday, and my gifts from Nick and Sylvie. About how Nick is so busy with Vanessa now, and Sylvie has been even more distracted than usual with Wendy and all her activities. I miss my friends, even though they're technically still around.

"Everything all right?" Dad asks me. Mom has slipped into the next room to assemble the desserts. Dad would rather have strawberry shortcake than birthday cake, so that's what we're having.

"Fine," I say automatically. Then: "Do you ever wish you lived closer to Benny, or closer to where you grew up?"

"Well, I'd like to see them all more often, Benny and my folks. But no, I don't want to live anywhere else. I know Benny always wanted to live closer to the water, where he could have a boat and go fishing all the time. And I always wanted to live out here where there's more trees and less traffic." He turns my box to face him, as if it's helping him think. "It's good you're getting out into the state parks, into the mountains. That's one reason I'm glad we live in this area. It's what I wanted, for my kid to be able to enjoy nature."

He should've seen me on Crystal Mountain, clutching the rock in terror. But all I say is, "I'm glad, too."

We look up as my mother carries in the dessert. "I've been asking Maggie to try some other activities," Mom says. "Not to spend so much time off in the woods. To get more involved at school."

"I like the woods," I say. "I belong there."

"Well, Maggie and I have just been discussing the importance of spending time where you belong," Dad says, smiling as he picks up his fork.

Mom holds up a hand. "Okay, okay. I'm just saying she should try something new. It would help with college, for one thing."

Dad steers us into a new subject, and while I'm thankful, underneath I know I still have to prove that I belong on Crystal.

When I imagine standing on its summit, the word that comes to me is *power*. The kind that rises from within and lets you know you control your own life. I flip back and forth between fear and anticipation, between believing it's where I need to be, and worrying that I can't make it.

I don't hear from Nick for most of the weekend, so I assume he's with Vanessa, especially since she talked all week about the various party-planning errands he was supposed to help her with. He calls me late on Sunday night, while I'm reading ahead in *Julius Caesar*. When my phone chirps, I answer it and snap off my lamp.

"I need a hike," Nick says.

"How about next Saturday? I'm ready to try Crystal again." I want to know what it's like to be on the trails with Nick again. If anything can close this distance between us, it will be a hike. And more than that, I want to feel strong again, to feel that sense of belonging on the trails.

"Great!" Nick says. "Don't worry. We'll start early, and we can go as slow as you want."

We talk for a while longer, and it's almost like the pre-Vanessa days. Now that we have a few minutes without Vanessa around, I even get to tell him what I've learned about Raleigh.

"Guess what I heard," I say, and launch into the story.

He's quiet for a minute. Then he says, "It must be nice to be able to run off to Italy whenever you have a problem."

"I wouldn't know."

He laughs. "And I would?"

"No. But I mean—I guess that story shows how she's still lucky in a lot of ways. But she's not as lucky as I thought she was. Or as smart. She would die if she thought I knew."

"I'm surprised more people don't know already. Her family must have connections. I'm sure if I helped somebody cheat, I'd be out on my ass before I could blink."

"Well, don't tell anyone, okay?"

"If that's what you want."

We are quiet, but neither of us moves to hang up.

"I should go," he says at last.

"Nick—"

"Yeah?"

Silence. He doesn't ask what I was going to say. I think we both know we have nothing more to say, that we just want to stay connected a little longer. When I can't put it off another moment, I say, "It's good to talk to you again."

"Same here," he says. It's another long minute before we say good-bye.

twenty-two

On Tuesday at lunch, Nick and Vanessa are not rubbing up against each other, or eating from each other's plates, or sneaking off to a quiet corner. When I sit down, they barely nod at me. Vanessa says to him, "I was *not* taking your father's side."

"You said he had a good point."

"Well, he did—*one* good point. That doesn't mean I agree with everything he said, or with how he said it."

"Vanessa, stay out of my family stuff."

"Oh, fine, Nick. Because you handle it *so well* on your own."

Nick picks up his sandwich and bites into it. I look down at my own sandwich, thinking that I should leave the table—but to go where?

"And speaking of families," she continues, "you could spend a little more time around mine."

"What's your problem now?"

"Why didn't you come over for dinner on Sunday? My

mother invited you, and you didn't come up with much of an excuse. And I wanted to go over the plans for the Halloween party. You said you'd help with that—"

"I am. I went with you to that party store way over in Cramer, and I told you I'd help you drag all those pumpkins to your house. . . ."

I hunch my shoulders, trying to make myself smaller.

"But you're acting like everything's a big chore, when this is supposed to be *fun.*"

"Sorry I don't live up to your high standards," Nick says. "You and my dad can get together and talk about how useless I am."

"Will you stop putting words in my mouth?"

"Between the two of you, I've got a list ten miles long of what's wrong with me. If I'm so worthless, why don't you walk away right now?"

"Nick, I can't take this anymore. Will you just—"

"Then *don't* take it. Like I said, walk away now."

She gapes at him. I concentrate on my sandwich, pretending I'm invisible. I might as well be, for all the attention they're paying me.

"What are you saying?" Vanessa asks. "Are you breaking up with me?"

"If that's what you want."

"I don't *believe* you," she mutters, picking up her tray. "You're impossible."

She stands there for a moment, as if waiting for him to ask

her to stay, but he stares straight ahead without saying anything. She walks over to her old table and sits with her back to us, next to Janie Fletcher.

"Anything I can do?" I say after a pause.

"Yeah," Nick answers. "Don't talk for the rest of lunch. Please."

"I can do that," I say, and we eat in silence.

"I'm sorry you had to see that at lunch," Vanessa says in French class, during a conversation exercise. We're supposed to discuss the price of fruit in an imaginary market, but our teacher is on the other side of the room. "I didn't mean for us to fight in front of you. It's just—I tried to have a simple discussion with him, and it went out of control. He wouldn't listen to reason. I can't believe he broke *up* with me over this."

"Well," I say slowly, "I didn't hear the whole thing, but it sounded like it started with something about his father, right?"

"Yes. His father was nagging him about schoolwork . . . and look, I know the guy is rude and pompous, and some of the stuff he says to Nick is pretty nasty. But he's right about one thing: Nick is smarter than he thinks, and he should set his sights higher. That's all I said. And he got so—"

"Nick's father has always been a sore point," I say. "I'm not sure I even know the whole story between them, but there's something Nick can't get over. I don't know if it's the divorce—

from what Nick says, it got very ugly—or the way his dad treats him, or what. But talking about Nick's dad with him is like—twisting a broken arm."

Vanessa ruffles her French book pages. "I don't know how things blew up so quickly. I didn't want to break up. Do you think he . . ."

The truth is, I don't believe Nick wanted to break up with her, either. I suspect he did that on impulse, and that he didn't mean half of what he said to her at lunch. But before I can say so, the teacher cruises past our desks. We launch into a few minutes of chatter about *cerises* and *framboises* and *bananes* until she moves on.

"Should I call him?" Vanessa asks.

"Well—"

"I kept trying to reason with him, and he wasn't ready to hear it. Everything I said made things worse."

"He'll cool down," I say.

"Or maybe—" She folds down the corner of a page, then flattens it again. I've never seen Vanessa so insecure. "Maybe you could talk to him. Just—encourage him to call me when he's ready to talk."

"Okay," I say, and we switch back to talking about how red the apples are, how fresh the grapes are, in our imaginary French market.

🍃 🍃 🍃

It's too rainy for outdoor basketball today. A tropical storm has blown into town, and it looks like it's going to hang over our heads all week.

The ringtone for Nick's father goes off as we get into the car after school, further clouding Nick's mood. He shuts off the phone without answering, but the atmosphere inside the car is unmistakably gloomy.

"What's with you, Cleary?" Luis says. "Whose funeral are we going to?"

"I thought driving you home every day was enough," Nick says. "I didn't know I had to entertain you the whole way, too."

It's probably supposed to come off as a joke, but his voice is so flat and cutting. The words smack me, and I know they must smack Luis. I rest a hand on Luis's shoulder, but he shrugs it off.

"If you don't want to drive me anymore, then hey, don't," Luis says.

"Sorry," Nick says.

"I can get home on my own."

"I didn't mean it like that. It's—kind of a screwed-up day." I don't know how much Nick has told Luis about his problems with his dad or about the breakup with Vanessa. Probably almost nothing, knowing Nick.

When we drop off Luis, he gives Nick a friendly nudge, an elbow-bump of forgiveness. The mood in the car lightens a little as I slide into the front seat, but I'm not exactly eager to ask Nick anything now. Not after the reception he gave Luis.

But I need to talk about our Crystal plan. And I think it

would help Nick, too. "Are you ready for Crystal on Saturday?" I say.

"I can't. My dad got my mom to change the schedule around, and now it's his weekend. *Again.*"

"Oh." Because Dr. Cleary's schedule is so weird (the proteins fold on their own timetable), he often switches around the visitation. Now I understand Nick's mood even better, and why he was so prickly at lunch. "That's too bad. But we can go the weekend after, right?"

Nick doesn't answer.

"Are you—okay?"

"Yeah, perfect. I'm having a *spectacular* day. My father calls fifteen times to tell me what a loser I am, he destroys my hiking plans, I break up with my girlfriend, and basketball gets rained out. Every time I turn around, the day gets better and better."

I say nothing. But I try to make my silence sympathetic.

"I'm sorry," he says. "I shouldn't take it out on you. Especially since you're the only person who can stand to be around me right now."

"That's not true," I say. "Luis is still your friend. There's your mom and Perry. And—" Maybe I should tell him about Vanessa. But I'm not sure that he's ready, that he has calmed down enough yet.

When he pulls up in front of my house, he takes out his phone and hits the button to check his messages. He holds up the phone so I can hear: "You have—thirteen—new messages."

"They'll all be from my dad," he says. "Thirteen calls, just on the ride over here. He'll be pissed that I sent him to voice mail."

I don't know what to say.

"Sounds like I'll be calling the Maggie Lifeline tonight," he says. "If you don't mind."

"I don't mind," I say. "I'll be there."

I'm struggling to read an extremely dry, repetitive essay about the domino theory for history class when Mom bursts into my room. "Phoebe called. Dr. Cleary wants to take Nick and a friend to dinner, and they want you to go."

"Nick's supposed to see his dad over the weekend. Not tonight."

"There's been some schedule change—his father can't make it on the weekend, so they're seeing each other tonight. In any case, if you want to go, it's all right with me."

"Okay." This means we can go to Crystal this weekend after all—assuming the tropical storm clears up. I toss aside my history book, relieved to put off the domino theory for a few hours. "Where are we going?"

"Midi." She fans herself. "My little girl is growing up. *I've* never even been to Midi!"

Yikes—I'll have to change. Even the bathroom attendants at Midi probably wear outfits that cost more than anything in my closet.

While Mom calls Phoebe, I dig out one of the two skirts I own, and pair it with a black shirt. Black is supposed to be sophisticated. Or so I've heard. I look at the ruffled shirt Mom gave me on my birthday, but it's white, and I can just picture a big food splotch on the chest before the night is over. The black will be better.

I pile my hair on top of my head, but decide it looks like a crow has nested up there. (*Heard of a comb, Maggie?* Raleigh once said.) I have no way to anchor it in place, anyway. Instead, I leave it long and attempt to fluff it out around my face. That will have to be good enough for Dr. Cleary and Midi.

I can't help thinking that Vanessa should be the one going with Nick, but I guess he's still angry with her. Since their whole fight started over her supposedly siding with his father, I don't imagine he's eager to bring them together right now.

My phone beeps. It's a text from Nick: **Thank you.**

twenty-three

Nick's wearing jeans and a T-shirt, but his father has on a crisp shirt and a jacket and tie. "You look pretty tonight, Margaret," Dr. Cleary says, and I would swear he emphasizes the word *tonight*, but I thank him and try to get Nick to look somewhere besides out the window.

Midi is rose-colored tablecloths and crystal and a menu full of words like *infused* and *shaved* and *confit*. Dr. Cleary spends ten minutes checking his messages, which I don't mind since it means we don't have to come up with conversation. Nick plays with his butter knife.

Dr. Cleary swirls the wine in his glass. "It needs to breathe," he says, staring expectantly at me.

"Oh," I reply. Demonstrating, in one word, my brilliant social skills and my intimate knowledge of wine.

Our conversation limps along with no help from Nick, who escapes to the men's room after the main course. I sip iced water from my goblet, hoping Nick's dad will go for his phone again. Instead, he says, "How was your shrimp, Margaret?"

"Good." And it was, but I wonder when I'll ever learn what to order at a fancy restaurant. I couldn't figure out how to get the tails off the shrimp without using my fingers. My napkin is smeared with the tomatoey broth the shrimp came in.

"My duck was a little dry," Dr. Cleary says. "It's usually excellent."

"Hm," I say. His eyes drift past me; he appears to be reading equations off the wall on the other side of the room. I get the feeling Dr. Cleary's mind never completely leaves his lab, a feeling that's only strengthened when his phone beeps.

"Yes," he says into the phone. "What? No, it has to go in by midnight. No. Where's Kieran? What? I don't want to hear it. I'll be right in."

He snaps off the phone and turns to check the men's room door, while I pray that Nick hasn't gone out the window. "Where is he?" Dr. Cleary mutters. "Margaret, I'm afraid I'll have to ask you to ride over to the lab with us before we drop you off. Something's come up that I have to deal with immediately."

"All right."

He marches to the men's room and puts his head in the door. Even from the table, I can hear him say, "Nick! Let's go!"

Dr. Cleary uses his ID badge to get us into the lab, swiping his plastic card through a series of beeping red electric eyes, pushing through door after door. We rush through a series of antiseptic corridors. When we reach his hall, he charges ahead of us down to his office, calling, "Sangita! Kieran!"

By the time Nick and I enter the office, Dr. Cleary is hunched over a computer with two of his researchers, their voices hushed. They focus so intently on the screen that it's like a movie in which they're trying to stop a missile from launching—though all they're really trying to do is launch a grant proposal.

They mutter to one another, stabbing at the keyboard, clicking buttons. "Make sure you have the latest versions of all the attachments," Dr. Cleary says, ice in his voice. Sangita sweeps a hand through her hair. Kieran's hair stands up all over his head.

"*No*," Dr. Cleary says. "Back up. There." He pokes a finger at the screen. "'Petide,' seriously? If you can't spell 'peptide,' you shouldn't even be working in this lab."

"It's just a typo," Kieran mumbles.

"Oh, brilliant. I'm sure they're looking for sloppy, lazy proposals that nobody could bother to spell-check."

Nick sits on a cardboard box beside his father's desk. I perch on a low step stool and try to arrange my skirt so that I'm not accidentally flashing anyone. The group in front of us taps away, flinging the occasional curt word at one another.

Sangita murmurs something, gesturing at the screen.

"No, that is *not* it," Dr. Cleary snaps.

"Yeah, it is," Kieran says.

"Kieran, pull your brain out of your ass and start using it. Get the right file up there."

"That is the right file. Three thirteen is the right file."

"Yes," Sangita says. "Noel and Fisher posted it this morning. Three thirteen is the latest."

Dr. Cleary wheels and stalks out of the room.

I glance at Nick, who gives me a dead, glazed look in return.

"You're welcome," Kieran says to the empty air where Dr. Cleary just stood. "'Oh, thank you, Kieran, yes, you're absolutely right. Three thirteen is right. I'm the one who's wrong. Thank you for pointing that out.'"

"Sshh," Sangita says. "Just pull up the rest of the files so we can get out of here."

Dr. Cleary stomps back in. "Three thirteen is the right file." With his eyes trained on the computer, he steps on Nick's foot. Nick jerks, knocking over a plastic cup on the desk. Pens, clips, and rubber bands spill across the desk, over the blotter and folders and stray papers. "Oh, that's a big help," Nick's father says.

The rest of us keep our mouths shut. At ten p.m., the proposal is sent, the researchers dismissed. Dr. Cleary sighs and begins sorting folders on his desk. Whenever he finds a clip or staple from the cup that Nick spilled, he flings it back into the holder, each one hitting with a hard, angry *ping*.

I've been thinking we're going to leave any minute, but neither Dr. Cleary nor Nick speaks, and the silence between them is so heavy that it steals my voice, too. But I can't wait another second for the ladies' room, so I slip out. We passed it on the way in; I know I can find it.

At this hour, the lab is almost deserted, the halls lit by bluish fluorescent ceiling squares. Every noise echoes, magnified. On my way back, I'm stopped just outside the office by Dr. Cleary's voice. His words pelt me through the half-open door.

"That's not what bothers me," he's saying. "It's that you seem perfectly happy with Bs. Even a C doesn't faze you. If I'd ever gotten a C in high school, I would've tried to hang myself."

"I'm not you," Nick says.

"That's all too obvious. You're heading for complete and total mediocrity. Is that what you want to be—a *nobody?*"

Nick doesn't answer.

"Then there's all that time you waste on basketball. You're not going to make the NBA, so why are you bothering? You're an average player on an average team. Study. That's your chance to do something with your life."

"You don't have to tell me again."

"Oh, really, Nick? Because I haven't noticed it sinking into your thick skull, no matter how many times I say it. That's what you have to do with stupid people: repeat things. Tell them over and over, until they finally start to get it. I've killed smarter cockroaches than you."

In the hall I stand, twining my fingers together, not knowing when to enter the room. I want to break this up, but I don't want Nick to know I've heard. And I don't know if I can be polite to his father right now. I want to rush in there and crush Dr. Cleary's huge arrogant head between my hands.

"Sometimes I wonder if you've sustained brain damage somewhere along the line," Nick's father says. "I don't know where it comes from. Your mother's not that stupid—"

"Leave her out of this." It's the first thing Nick has said with any pulse of life in it. Until now, he has sounded almost as if he's been reading from cue cards. I get the feeling these two have had this conversation many times before.

"I give up. I can't even stand the sight of you right now."

I expect Nick to say, "It's mutual," but the room is silent. After a minute, shuffling noises suggest that Dr. Cleary has returned to cleaning his desk, and I walk in.

"Margaret," Dr. Cleary says. "Are you ready to leave?"

As if *I've* been the one keeping us here all night. I'm afraid my face must be red with fury. Knotting my hands together, not looking at Nick or his father, I say, "Yes, you can take me to Nick's. My mom will pick me up there on her way home."

Mom's not actually working tonight, and it would be simpler for Dr. Cleary to take me home. But there's no way I'm letting Nick go home alone with his father's words ringing in his head.

Nick and I don't talk to each other. But in the backseat of the car, I slip my hand into his, and he grasps it as if I might vanish otherwise. Aside from one polite sentence to thank Dr. Cleary for dinner, I am quiet, every cell of me focused on the moment when I can be alone with Nick.

We're in Nick's room. I kick off my fussy, pinching shoes and swap my "nice" (that is, stiff and uncomfortable) shirt for one of Nick's T-shirts. We leave his light off, relying only on the streetlight glow coming in the window.

I think Phoebe and Perry suspected something was wrong when we walked in the door. "How was dinner?" they kept asking, as if detecting the tension hidden in Nick's blank expression, the truth buried in his monotone "Fine." Perry paced, the way he always does when he wants to fix something, as if itching to physically put his hands on the problem. Phoebe turned from Nick to me in what I thought of as a flanking maneuver. "*Was* it 'fine,' Maggie?"

"Yes," I said with Nick's eyes fastened on my face. "Midi is beautiful."

But now that we're alone, I'm determined to get Nick to talk to me.

We lie on his bed as we've done a thousand times before, although this time his father floats in an ominous cloud over our heads. I'm not sure Nick knows I heard what Dr. Cleary said to him, but I can't pretend that I didn't.

"Your father's wrong," I say.

Nick tenses; the room temperature seems to fall ten degrees. But I push on.

"He was being totally unrealistic. He sees the world one narrow way, and—"

"Maggie," Nick cuts in, "don't tell me how my father is." He sits up and leans his back against the headboard.

"You're right. What am I telling you for? You already know he's way off base."

"I know I'm not smart," he says. "I just wish he didn't have to rub it in all the time. Like, since I'm not a genius, I'm a waste."

"You are smart. Don't listen to him. You're seventeen, and he's trying to compare you to world-famous scientists."

"He compares me to himself," Nick says. "There's no way I'm ever going to win that one."

I squeeze his arm.

"I used to think it would get better, that he'd ease up or I'd get smarter, but instead it gets worse every year. 'If I got a C, I would hang myself.' What the hell?"

"What does your mom say? I know she doesn't believe—"

"She doesn't know. I mean, she knows he thinks he's God's gift to the world, but she doesn't know how bad he's gotten. He used to talk about other stuff with me and just lecture me once in a while. He took me fishing and to movies and museums sometimes. Now all he does is tell me what a moron I am."

"You should tell her."

"No."

"Why not? She'd want to know that—"

"You didn't see that divorce, Maggie. She went through five lawyers. She got served papers every time she walked out into the driveway. They itemized everything in the house, down to the forks and spoons. She used to puke every time she had to go to court."

It's true, I didn't see the divorce. Nick was about eight then; I didn't know him yet.

"If she thinks I'm having problems with him, she might get

some crazy idea in her head about trying to change the custody agreement. Which means more lawyers, more papers. I'm not putting her through that." He coughs. "In six months, I'll be eighteen and it'll be easier. There's no point stirring things up now."

His voice roughens on that last sentence, cracking to reveal hunger underneath. It reminds me of the look on his face when he used to show his father basketball trophies and better-than-usual report cards, all the things he once brought to Dr. Cleary for approval, before he learned how futile it was. And I realize, despite everything, Nick doesn't *want* to stop seeing his father. Which is maybe the most painful part of all.

I stroke his arm.

"This has been a hell of a day," Nick says. He takes out his phone and checks the messages. "Should I call Vanessa?" he asks, his eyes still on the screen.

"Why?" I ask. Maybe I should've said yes right away, but I tell myself I'm trying to help him figure out exactly what he wants.

"She hasn't called me," he says as if I haven't spoken. "Do you think I should call her?"

"Not if you're still mad."

"I'm not. But she probably is. I don't know."

I should tell him. Right now, I should tell him she wants him to call. But the words refuse to come out.

He puts away the phone and lies back down next to me. I let go of his arm. We stare up at his ceiling, but I'm very aware of his warmth, an inch or two away. "You know those glow-in-the-dark stars you can put on your ceiling?" he says.

"Yeah."

"I had them when I was little, at our old house, when my parents were still together. Dad said we should put them in exactly the right spots to mimic the real constellations, but I wanted to make my own galaxy. So I stuck them up there in a pattern I invented myself. He went ballistic."

"You're *supposed* to have fun with those stars," I say.

"To him, it was like I was insisting that two plus two is five, or that the Earth is square. He didn't even talk to me for a week."

"Jeez," I say, "the guy doesn't bend *at all*, does he?"

Nick laughs a little.

"Did he let you have toy dinosaurs, or did they have to be exact scale-model replicas of real dinosaurs?"

Nick laughs again, which makes me laugh, which makes him laugh more. And then we're both laughing so hard that the bed shakes, and we gasp for breath. Beneath it runs a sad horror; we know there's something profoundly unfunny about the bitterness between Nick and his father. But laughing still feels good, releasing the tension that's been growing through the whole night.

Our laughter subsides, leaving behind the glow of connection. I squeeze his hand, and he squeezes back.

"Hey," he says, "I should bring you along every time I have to see him."

"The Maggie Lifeline goes live and in person." I drop his hand and turn toward him, rolling onto my side, at the same moment he turns toward me.

Our skin is shadow-gray in the dim light, his mouth dark and achingly close. For a breathless minute I'm sure he's going to kiss me again.

He doesn't bend toward me. But he doesn't pull away, either.

"Thanks," he says. "For coming with me tonight."

"I was glad to."

He looks away from my face, chuckling as his eyes sweep over the T-shirt he lent me. He touches my side, rubbing a loose fold of cloth. "This is really big on you."

"And here I thought I was making a bold fashion statement."

Our eyes meet again, the heat between us building and building, his hand resting lightly on the side of my rib cage. Neither of us moves. But then I have to, because the arm I'm lying on has fallen asleep. As soon as I shift my weight, he pulls his hand back. He turns his head away. I'm trying to work up the nerve to reach out to him when my phone beeps. It's my mother, calling me home.

twenty-four

For the rest of the week, Nick and Vanessa avoid each other, though I catch each of them sneaking looks at the other. I wonder if Vanessa is the reason Nick didn't kiss me in his room after Midi, even though I'd thought he wanted to. I can't forget him checking his phone that night, asking me if he should call her. And there's no mistaking the way his eyes follow her when she crosses the cafeteria to sit with Janie Fletcher.

Maybe it's crazy of me to hope that they're truly finished with each other. I should tell at least one of them that the other wants to talk—maybe that's all it would take for them to fix the split between them—but I can't force those words out.

I text Sylvie a million times so that she can tell me do the right thing.

Am I a bad person for not wanting Nick and Vanessa to get back together?

I really do want Nick to be happy.

It's nice not having to watch her glue her lips to his face though.

But I don't want to be petty, either. If they belong together . . .

Then again, sometimes I think he might like me.

What should I do?

Do you want to get together and talk?

Sylvie doesn't seem to want to help me with my soul searching. When I catch her on the phone on Friday, she says wearily, "What is it this time, Maggie?"

"Oh, uh—nothing. I wondered if you've been getting my messages."

"Yes, of course. I haven't had time to answer you. Things are complicated around here. . . ."

"Well, do you have any advice? I'm driving myself crazy trying to figure this out."

"Just do whatever you think is right." Her words are automatic, stiff. Even though she says she's getting my messages, I wonder if she's *reading* them.

"That's the trouble: I don't *know* what's right. I keep changing my mind. It's not like I can be objective about this."

"I'm sorry, Maggie. I'm kind of distracted by some stuff going on with Wendy, and I—can we catch up later?"

"Well—okay . . ."

She says a hurried thanks before hanging up. Leaving me alone with this same problem, spinning in the same old spot.

The piano doesn't have any answers for me, either, though I go to it anyway, playing "Nightwaves," playing fast and complicated pieces that require concentration. I keep hoping that if I distract my conscious mind, some deeper part of my brain will come up with a solution and jump out of the darkness, waving the answer in my face. *This is what you should do!* But it doesn't happen.

There's also the upcoming hike to worry about, my second chance at Crystal. For that I play slow, powerful music, anything that sounds like confidence to me.

By the time Nick and I set out for our return to Crystal Mountain, he and Vanessa still haven't worked up the nerve to talk to each other, and I haven't said anything to either of them. I tell myself it's their own business; it's not my job to fix their relationship. My job is to see if I can make it up this mountain. Or at least past the point where I froze last time.

On Friday night, at Nick's, I keep the conversation to practical things: our route up Crystal, the weather we expect, the food we'll bring. I'm up before six on Saturday, packing my gear under electric-light glare. The sky outside is black. I double-check that I have all my gear, using the checklist Perry once gave me, packing extras of everything.

This time, I don't have to drag Nick out of bed. He meets me in the kitchen: uncombed and bleary-eyed, clutching a mug of coffee, but awake.

"I'm guessing it'll be windy at the top," he says as we climb into the car.

"Maybe." It's hard to believe, since the air is calm right now, so peaceful that Nick and I might be the only people alive. But that tropical storm has been stirring up the atmosphere all week, and Perry has warned us about the weirdness of mountain weather, about breaking through tree line to get slapped in the face by wind.

Nick shifts out of PARK, his knuckles paling as he grips the knob. I focus on his hand to keep from looking at the rest of him. To keep from thinking about the rest of him.

But I have a more immediate problem: getting past those ledges that stopped me before. I don't want to be weak. Weak gets walked on. Weak is how Raleigh saw me, and the last thing in the world I want is to see myself through her lens, to believe that anything she said about me was right. If I don't belong out here—on the mountain, in the woods—then I don't belong anywhere; there's no room for me in the world.

The first highway sign for Crystal Mountain is tilted today, probably blown crooked by the recent storm, and I tell myself not to take it as a bad omen. My legs twitch, and I jiggle them to keep the muscles loose. I stare out the windshield as the car eats up the miles, heading north to the Cinnamon Range.

twenty-five

When we step onto the Crystal trail once again, I have to admit that those hikers in the online forum weren't joking about the rocks. They're not evenly spaced, so every step is different, and it's a struggle to stay balanced. I have to watch my feet instead of the world around me. I slip and stumble, and Nick slips and stumbles. Our experience doesn't help us here: it's just as hard the second time around.

We find plenty of bare rock still coated with wet leaves from the week's storm. The leaves form a slippery pulp on which our boots skid.

Sometimes climbing hurts so much I wonder why I do it: the strain in my legs, the soreness in my feet, the scrape of twigs against my face. After our first few hikes, Nick and I did the "Frankenstein shuffle," hobbled by stiffness for a couple of days. (Even so, Perry used to say, as he grabbed various muscle wraps and ointments, "Boy, you kids bounce back quickly. Wait until you're my age.")

But today, on the lower slopes of Crystal, sunlight touches a clump of lacy ferns with a gentleness that makes me glad I'm alive to see it. Dead leaves give off an earthy fragrance, and I find mushrooms to identify along the trail.

Even Nick's silence is okay right now, because we're usually pretty quiet when we hike. This quiet is sharper, more jagged than usual, but for now I can get away with pretending that it's our usual comfortable silence. Pretending that Vanessa doesn't haunt the space between us.

About halfway up, we start catching views. We stand on a rocky knob, panting, looking out over a valley with tiny houses and a greenish circle of lake. I use the scissors in my knife to trim a piece of moleskin for my left heel, to keep a hot spot there from turning into a blister. Nick helps me smooth it over my skin.

Above us rises the rest of Crystal. "There's our high point from last time," Nick says, nodding at the ledges still ahead.

"My Waterloo," I say in a voice deliberately melodramatic, and Nick laughs.

That laughter breaks some icy dread within me. I had decided to be brave, to pretend I'm not scared out of my mind. But who am I putting on a front for? Nick was here. He saw what happened.

"Onward and upward," he says. In this moment, our old connection is back: our pre-kiss, pre-Vanessa link. I follow him without a word, not wanting to break the spell.

🍃 🍃 🍃

We reach the base of the exposed ledges. "Okay," Nick says. "Do you want to go first, or do you want me to?"

"I'll go."

I make sure my backpack's snug so it won't slip around and throw me off balance. There's so much *air* up here. Fears shout inside my head. I picture myself wheeling through the air, my neck cracking, skull smashing, spinal column snapping.

I gather myself, summoning every mental trick I've ever come up with: Breathe deeply and slowly. Take one step at a time. Pretend I'm setting my boots down squarely on Raleigh Barringer's face.

I force myself to concentrate on the position of my hands and feet, on the ground in front of me. I pick my way up through the first section, finding the dimples and bumps in the rock. I test each inch of ground before I put my full weight on it, avoiding the least stable footholds. After the first few steps, I don't glance down, but I know Nick is there below me. Spider-like, I creep upward, occasionally bending forward to use my hands. *This step, this step, next step, you can do it, you can do it*, I chant to myself.

Vertigo shoots through me, a sickening downward rush. An inner voice screams, *Get me out of here, Maggie!*

I know how to counter that voice. *Shut up!* I tell it. *You can do this! You are doing this!*

My every handhold is a death grip. The rock leaves red dents in my skin. Sweat mats my hair to my head, collects under my jacket, and trickles down my back. But every step is a miracle, my feet doing what I thought was impossible.

Above the ledges, I find a wide, flat, mossy spot. I fling myself down on it, panting. Nick climbs steadily toward me. Tears fill my eyes, but I blink until I can see clearly again.

I've done it. I've passed my high point.

Nick grins when he reaches my mossy perch, and pushes his palm toward me, fingers spread wide. I slap his hand in triumph. We don't even comment on what I've just done.

"What's next?" I say.

We're supposed to climb through a waterfall.

This is not what you usually picture when you hear the word *waterfall*. It's not a sheer curtain of water pouring off a ledge. It's a set of rocky steps with spring water burbling down them, just enough water to keep the rock wet and slippery. I would hunt for another way around if the trees and bushes on either side weren't impenetrably thick, their branches weaving together, hemming us in.

"Oh, great," Nick says, surveying it.

"Yeah," I say.

It would be all right if the rocks we had to step on were flat and stable. But they're not. They're angled; they're pointy. Or they wobble, or the distance between one rock and the next is slightly farther than I can step. And every one of them is slick with leaves, mud, or moss. Nick and I slide and splash and curse, steadying ourselves on trees and rocks.

"What'd the guidebook say about this?" he asks.

"'A tricky section that may be especially hazardous in wet weather.'"

"Lucky us, to climb the week after a tropical storm." He yelps with laughter as his feet slide again. "Are we having fun yet?"

Gasping, grimy, we come to the last section before the top. This is a series of boulders set between wind-stunted trees. There's nothing especially tough about it except that we know we're close to the summit, and although we keep climbing, we never seem to get any closer.

Our progress up the rocks is slow. We want to dash up there, eat up the ground in a few leaps, but in order to keep from twisting an ankle—or cracking our skulls—we have to inch forward, balancing, sensibly securing each hold before seeking the next. I try to ignore the feeling that I'm mincing along like an old lady with hemorrhoids.

"I hate to say it," Nick says, "but we might make it this time."

"Hey! Don't jinx it."

"Or we might be stuck in an alternate universe where we climb forever without getting anywhere."

The rock roughens my hands, but the hours of climbing

have warmed me. I'm finally friends with this mountain, after the last trip where it spat me out like rancid food. I read the stone, swing my body into position, and move up, over and over again. Nick moves with no hesitation or fumbling, with an ease that's almost magical, and I sense that he's also found the rhythm of Crystal.

Another hiker puffs toward us, descending. "Heading up to the summit?" he asks. His face is red. His few strands of hair have all blown to one side of his head.

"Yeah. How is it up there?" Nick asks.

"Windy. It's incredible. I'm guessing forty, fifty miles an hour."

It's our first warning that Nick's prediction about the wind might be right. It's hard to imagine, since we're sheltered here, with only the slightest breeze making it past the neighboring peaks and through the trees.

But above tree line, there will be nothing to block the wind, nothing except our own strength to keep it from sweeping us off the mountain.

As promised, the wind picks up as soon as we break through the trees. I stop to twist my hair into a clumsy braid. Stray wisps blow around my face, but at least I won't be blinded by my own hair.

Blazes painted on the rock, splashes of blue, lead us on a winding trail toward the top of the peak. The sun throws sharp shadows onto the ground. No longer surrounded by trees, we can see the land below us: other mountains, their trees puffs of green, red, and yellow; toy farms with patchwork fields; a silver ribbon of river.

The higher we climb, the fiercer the wind gets, rising from a whisper to a moan to a roar. It blasts us wherever the trail changes direction. It whips my braid around and makes our jackets snap furiously. Tears trickle from my eyes, but I'm afraid to let go of the rock long enough to wipe them away. Nick shouts something I can't hear.

We claw our way upward, though I ask myself if we should stop. The hiker ahead of us made it—he didn't get blown off the top—but this wind feels like the very edge of what's safe. If it strengthens the slightest bit, it might blow us off.

We're so close. The summit of Crystal is within reach. After fighting myself to make it this far, I'm practically *there*.

The wind increases with every step upward. My eyes leak water; my nose drips. I want to grab on to the mountain and just stay still for a minute, but I'm afraid to lose momentum. If I freeze like last time, who knows when I'll be able to unglue myself from the rock?

My breathing gets wilder, a desperate panting. I follow Nick not only because I don't know what else to do, but also because something deep inside me still wants to reach the top, to finish what I've started.

We arrive at a flat spot right below the summit. From a distance, Crystal's top looks sharp and fanglike, as in the picture in Nick's room. But up close, we find that the official top is a round hump of rock, exposed on all sides to the punishing wind. I sit with my back against the summit rock, feet planted on the flat ground. Nick yells, "Come on, Maggie!" in my ear, but I hold up one finger to say, *Give me a minute.*

He pushes himself up the bald curve of the summit rock, and then he's there—on his hands and knees, but there. He lets out a howl of joy that I can hear even over the roaring wind.

I want to be there, I ache to be there, but the wind pummels me and steals my breath. It's savage, relentless. Hysteria rises in my throat.

Nick waves at me.

I need to do this. I can't stand the thought of failing—not now, so close. If Nick is up there, then it's possible for me to be up there, too, right? It's not really the wind that can stop me now; it's my fear of the wind, my own twisted mind.

I crawl to the base of the summit rock.

I get as low as possible, to make it harder for the wind to blow me off. And I creep up that rock on my belly, clinging to it with every stone-scraped skin cell. Below me: solid rock. Above me: miles of empty air, stretching up to outer space, a vast nothingness where the wind wants to hurl me.

Nick reaches down to me, and I crawl toward his outstretched fingers. I hitch myself forward, inchworm-style, in what is probably the least graceful summiting of this mountain ever, but—

I'm here.

On the top.

Of Crystal.

I lie on my stomach, afraid that if I rise the slightest bit, the wind will peel me off and fling me from the mountain.

But we've made it.

Nick touches my back. He might be laughing at the way I'm gripping the mountain, my face pressed to the stone, but I don't care.

The power of wind and rock and air and sun flow through me. People talk about having a sense of forces bigger than themselves—well, this is it. Right here. All my life, I've never known, the way I know now, how small I am. A speck on the face of the earth.

Nick taps my shoulder and we crab-step over the top, the wind pounding us. We'll take the orange trail down. Nick's black hair flies in the wind. I brush a hand across my face to clear away the water running from my eyes.

The top of a mountain is only the halfway point. Gravity and the slope of Crystal pull on me. Heaviness and vertigo tempt me to plunge all the way back down to sea level. I move one step at a time, clasping rock wherever possible to keep myself grounded, not airborne.

🍃 🍃 🍃

We stop just below tree line. The wind subsides, and I free my hair from its braid, pushing stray strands out of my face. "We did it," Nick says, grinning.

"We're not down yet."

He laughs. Together we sink onto a mossy rock, legs sprawling, for a good rest. He paws through his pack and pulls out a chocolate-covered granola bar. I love those things. He tosses me one before I even have to ask.

I wash down the chocolate and oats with water from my bottle, thinking that this is my first meal on the other side of Crystal. The first food of "the rest of my life." Would Nick laugh if I told him that? The way he's rolling the food around in his mouth, relishing every bite, somehow I don't think he would.

"Do you think today was worse than Eagle?" he says.

"Well, Eagle was slippery, but at least I could *stand up*. Today, I thought the wind would knock me right off the mountain."

He leans into me, lets his shoulder bump mine. "You did it, though. I thought I was going to have to drag you up that last stretch, but you did it."

I laugh. "I'm not proud about crawling, but you do what you gotta do." I run my fingers through my knotted hair, trying to tame it, and some of it brushes Nick's cheek. Smiling, he flips the strands back at me and bumps my shoulder again. I bump him back. Warmth floods me: the warmth of climbing Crystal, tasting chocolate, watching sunlight peek between tree branches and dapple the ground. The warmth of being close to Nick.

I don't have words for it, this happiness. I take his hand and squeeze it, as if I can get him to understand that way. But I haven't thought this through, and I'm not prepared for the heat that travels up my arm when he squeezes back. He's still full of the summit, his skin sending off triumphant sparks.

I trace his mouth with my eyes. Wondering what he would do if I leaned in now.

I angle toward him, not in an obvious kissing position but in what I think of as a "kissing-accessible" position. He doesn't move away.

If anything, he leans a shade closer.

So I tip up my chin and touch my lips to his.

hold my mouth against Nick's for a full second, giving him the chance to draw away. He doesn't.

Instead, he kisses me back, his tongue twining with mine. Guilt and fear boil in my stomach, but joy is there, too. The feeling that I'm finally making this right, that this time I'm not running away.

But in the back of my mind, I can't help wondering if Vanessa was better at this than I am. If maybe she had special make-out secrets, which he misses right now.

It's a long minute before he breaks away from me, gasping a little. "Where'd that come from?"

"I—" I brush my forehead, where sweat has sprung up, gluing wisps of hair to my skin. "I've been wanting to do that for a while."

He shakes his head. I can't tell if he's denying what I've said or trying to clear his mind. "Not a few weeks ago, you didn't."

"No, I—" I clear my throat. "Look, Nick. I only ran away

that day because it threw me off when your mom came home. I didn't know what to do. I was nervous, and I . . ." My heart pounds; my eyeballs throb with every beat. I'm floundering, but I can't back out now. "It was exactly what I wanted. It was so good I couldn't even handle it; I was too excited. But then you didn't call me." I swallow. "I figured you weren't interested after all. That you'd made a mistake."

"Oh," he says. Blank. Neutral. I'm not sure he has digested my words yet.

"I thought, well—at least I could keep you as a friend. And maybe it would even be easier. Safer. But . . ." I try to laugh. It sounds as if a fork is stuck in my throat. "Turns out it hasn't been so easy after all."

It's like my heart is sitting in the palm of my hand, pulpy and bloody, dripping onto the ground while I wait for him to reach out for it.

Or not.

He wipes his mouth. Then he scoops pebbles off the ground, holds them as if they're tiny birds' eggs. Flecks of mica glint in the sun.

"You did like me back then, right?" My mouth is so dry it creaks.

He makes a short noise, not quite a laugh. "Since the summer."

"Why?" I whisper. Because even with the lingering feel of his kiss on my lips, I still can't believe it. It's Raleigh's voice in my head: *No boy could ever like you.*

He shrugs. "When we started hiking alone, after Perry had to quit . . . I kept noticing how much I liked it. That it wasn't just the trails—it was you, too. The way we got along, we always had fun. And I wanted to see you more and more . . . but I couldn't tell if it was just on my side, or what."

My stomach leaps. So he liked me even before my birthday, the afternoon in his room when I'd felt the first spark between us. I hadn't been imagining the impossible.

"By the time we went to Eagle, I thought you felt the same way. But then you ran away from me, and you said forget about it."

He opens his hand and lets the pebbles fall. "And then there was Vanessa."

"Oh. Yeah. Vanessa." I struggle to keep my voice even, not to squeak. "But that's over, right?"

"I don't know if it is. Not for me, anyway."

It's like a punch to the throat.

He gets up and walks a tight circle, watching his boots on the ground.

"Do you really like her, Nick?"

"Is that why you're so interested now? Because she's around?"

My eyes drop. I guess I know why he would think this. I told him I wanted to be just friends, nothing more . . . and then when he started seeing her, I couldn't keep my jealousy from leaking out. But it's hard to explain how tangled up I've been, this push-pull of fear and attraction.

"She's nice," he says. "She knows what she wants. She doesn't play these head games with me."

"I wasn't playing games with you. I was confused myself."

"If you say so."

He steps toward me until his boots fill my field of vision. Mud clings to the toes and the edges of the soles. The laces look like he's chewed them. The leather is creased but not cracked, the mesh parts grimy but intact. Nick uses his boots hard but he takes care of them, too.

"Nick," I say, "this isn't—I'm not being the possessive friend here, trying to get you to play on my swing set again." I pull at the broad straps on my backpack. "Should I shut up? I mean, if you're really not interested in me anymore—"

"I just—I don't know. I need to think."

He stands at a gap between the trees, staring out at the view. I gulp water, sitting alone on my rock. *He kissed me back, just a few minutes ago*, I remind myself, trying to draw hope from it. And it is hopeful. Until I realize that here we are, talking about Vanessa.

I need to tell him what she said about him. Even though I'd rather do anything else—I'd rather get stuck in an elevator with Raleigh Barringer. But it's not fair to hold back. If he makes a choice, then I want it to be a real choice, not based on me hiding information from him.

"Vanessa wants to get back together with you," I say.

He turns his head toward me, but I can't read his expression.

"She's been wanting you to call."

"How do you know?"

"She told me a couple of days ago."

"Why didn't you tell me before?"

Isn't it obvious? "Because I'm jealous, that's why!" I squeeze the straps on my pack. "But I'm trying to do the right thing here."

He walks over to his backpack and picks it up. "You ready to head down?"

"I'm sorry," I say.

He nods, buckling his straps.

"What do you—I mean, what are you going to—"

"Maggie, I'm going to concentrate on getting down this mountain. This is a lot to get hit with at once, you know?"

I hoist my pack onto my shoulders and fall in beside him. We don't speak, which isn't unusual for us, but this time the air buzzes with unsaid things.

get home to find a distraction from the whole Nick problem: my application to be a student member of the "Hands-
on Conservation" program has been accepted. I can start by
showing up at a park cleanup on October 27. There's a sheaf
of forms I'm supposed to bring with me: parental permission
slip, insurance and liability form, medical form listing my aller-
gies and medications. There's also a list of equipment I need
to bring, which is practically an inventory of the contents of
my backpack. Reading it gives me my first stir of excitement,
the same anticipation as preparing for a hike: STURDY BOOTS,
WORK GLOVES, HAT, RAIN SUIT, WATER BOTTLES (WATER WILL BE
PROVIDED) . . .

I print out the forms and bring them downstairs. Mom is
sorting through a box of old clothes, including several extra
Mid-Regional POWER T-shirts.

"Do you want one of these?" she asks.

I've never taken one before, but now my embarrassment

over the logo seems silly. After being on the summit of Crystal, my threshold for self-consciousness has crept upward. "Sure," I tell her.

"Here's an extra-large. Do you think Nick might want it?"

I want to say, "I have no idea what Nick wants," but rather than get into that, I go with, "Maybe. I'll see."

She tosses both shirts at me and eyes the papers in my hand. "What's all that?"

"You said to get involved in activities. So this is what I picked."

She shuffles through them. "Maggie, this isn't a school club."

"It's still an activity I can put on my college applications. Besides, I want to do it."

She reads the forms, a frown puckering her face. And then she looks up at me. I can feel her eyes tracing my windblown hair, sweatshirt with frayed collar, dusty jeans. In spite of her telling me to socialize more, I have just come from another hike alone with Nick. This conservation group will also mean running off to the woods. It's not any of the activities she suggested: drama club, newspaper. I'm not exactly doing this her way.

I can almost hear the questions coming, the instructions to redo this or do it differently. Like my college-visit list all over again. But something—the thrill of climbing Crystal at last? The nerve it took to kiss Nick?—straightens my spine. We stare at each other a minute.

"Where's a pen?" she says.

"What?"

She leaves the box of clothes and hunts in the kitchen drawer until she finds a pen. She signs all the forms, her enthusiasm rising with each one. "This is wonderful, Maggie," she says. "You'll get to meet new people. It looks like fun."

"Hard work, too."

"Well, yes, but you seem to like doing things with your hands. Piano, and woodworking, and so forth . . . I'm sure you can do it. They say here they'll train you."

I wasn't sure she would be excited about an idea she didn't come up with herself. And I'm even more grateful for her support after hearing Dr. Cleary tell Nick that he's brain damaged and stupider than a cockroach.

"I'll need you or Dad to drive me over to this park and pick me up," I say. "Maybe when I get to know people, there'll be someone to carpool with. And Dad said he'll start teaching me to drive this fall. But for now—"

"That shouldn't be a problem. One of us will be free, I'm sure."

Well. Maybe if she's underestimated me, I've underestimated her, too.

I go upstairs and reread the list of equipment, savoring each item the way I savor the names of mushrooms.

The thought of starting something new with people I've never met scares me, but excitement peeks out from under a layer of nervousness. We'll be in the woods, with the scent of pine and the chatter of birds and the silent sturdiness of trees.

This program is the kind of thing Nick would probably like to do as well, but I can't bring myself to send him the information. I don't know where we stand with each other right now.

I start writing him several messages, but erase each one before I can finish.

In Nick's car Monday morning, we don't say much, but that's not unusual. Nick wakes up enough to operate the car. Conversation is an extra effort that Luis and I have learned not to expect at this hour.

"Heard you climbed another mountain," Luis says to me. I can't completely squash the glow that comes with saying, "Yes," even though Nick stays silent while I sketch for Luis, in a few sentences, the danger of the ledges, the force of the wind at the Crystal summit.

Between second and third periods, I'm at my locker when Vanessa comes up behind me.

"Bitch," she says, and I jump.

"What?" I say over my shoulder.

"You, Margaret Camden, are a bitch," she repeats. Slowly, clearly. Tasting each letter. "I can't believe how two-faced you are."

"What's your problem?" I cannot get the sleeves of my coat

to fit in the locker. They keep snagging on the door catch, so I leave them alone and turn to face Vanessa.

"My problem? *You're* the one with a problem. I told you I wanted to make up with Nick. I even asked you to help me. And instead, you threw yourself at him?"

"I didn't throw—"

"You've been friends with Nick for years, but it's not until he's with me that you *suddenly* get this uncontrollable urge for him? Come on."

I struggle to stand my ground, not to shrink into the locker behind me. I grip the open door, and its metal edge bites into my hand. "It wasn't sudden," I begin, but she cuts me off.

"He asked you if he should call me. And instead of telling him, 'Yes, that's exactly what she wants,' you tried to get him for yourself. It's disgusting. You went behind my back—acting so innocent with me, while the whole time you were planning to go after Nick."

"No, it's not like that. I—"

"Nick and I talked it out during first period. So don't even try to lie anymore. I know who you *really* are now." She storms away, and I sink against the row of lockers.

I hate having people mad at me.

Things never turn out well when people are mad at me.

The words *bitch* and *disgusting* ring in my ears—words Raleigh and Adriana used against me. For a minute, I'm back in junior high: My ears tuned to every whisper. My eyes scanning the hall. Holding my breath every time I turn a corner. I can't stand living with razors in my stomach, always wondering what's coming next. I can't go through that again.

But worse than anything, this time, is that Nick might be part of it.

Does he hate me, too, now that he's talked with Vanessa? She obviously believes I plotted this whole thing. When the truth is I've just been bumbling around, saying the wrong thing at the wrong time, never believing I have the power to hurt anyone—not weak, ugly, clumsy me. But if she thinks this was a scheme, it means Nick either couldn't convince her that it wasn't—or he believes it now, too.

I sit on the floor and text him. I don't know when he'll get this since he rarely checks his phone before lunch, but I'm desperate to reach him any way I can. **I need to talk to you.**

Then I text Sylvie. When she doesn't beep me back right away, I text her again. **Need to talk, URGENT!**

I keep my eyes down and hurry to study hall, knowing that to risk eye contact with anyone is to ask for disaster.

In study hall I take out my mushroom guide and bend over it, determined not to look at anyone else, not to leave myself open.

I don't know why I thought I could get away with this, that I could steal some happiness.

What is Vanessa going to do now? Try to keep me from Nick, obviously, but—will she stop there? Or will it be like junior high all over? Vanessa knows a lot of people. Her parties are famous. People look up to her. They would follow her if she wanted to rally them.

Not this again please God not this again not this . . .

Enough. I'm reading about mushrooms. Carmine coral. Indigo lactarius. Collared earthstar. I shield my face between my hands and whisper the names, roll them around on my tongue, trying to drown out the panicked voice in my head. Trying to fill the gaping space left by Nick.

I flip to the poisonous, powerful ones again: the haymaker's mushroom, red-mouth bolete, deadly galerina. And the one I see as the queen of the killers: the destroying angel. That is the one nobody messes with, ever.

'm alert in the halls and the bathrooms, but nobody comes after me. Not yet.

When it's time for lunch, I don't go into the cafeteria. I can't face Nick and Vanessa by myself.

Instead, I find the room where Sylvie is at a club meeting. I stand outside the door, signaling frantically until she sees me and slips out.

"What is it?" she says. She closes the classroom door, and we walk a few steps away from it.

I blurt out the story, ending with, "And now Nick and Vanessa hate me. What am I going to do?"

She rubs one eye and stares at the lockers across the hall. "I don't know, Maggie."

"I can't go into that cafeteria alone. Would anyone mind if I sat in your meeting? I won't say anything. I'll sit in the back. Or maybe we could go somewhere else and talk?"

Her eyes return to my face. "You mean, you want me to

listen to you." Her voice is sharper than usual, her face harder.

"I guess so." I don't understand what's wrong. Sylvie has an endless capacity to listen, a bottomless well of patience. But now she looks—tired. Puffy-eyed. As if she's been up all night.

"You ask me to listen a lot," she says. "And I do. But lately, you don't listen much to me. You don't even know what I'm going through right now."

"What? What are you going through?"

"Wendy and I broke up this weekend."

"Oh . . . Why didn't you tell me?"

"Because you never gave me room to tell you. This has been coming for a while. I told you Wendy was acting distant, and I told you I was worried—" Her voice breaks. "But you didn't *hear* me. All you ever talk about is your own problems. God, you're so needy, Maggie!" She closes her eyes and presses her palms against the lids. "My eyes are killing me. I was up crying all night and—I'm sorry. I shouldn't be talking to you this way. I should try to find a nicer way to say it. But I'm just—sick and tired and—I have no energy to deal with you right now."

Her mouth puckers, as if she might cry again, but I can't see her eyes. Only the backs of her hands.

"Sylvie—"

"Leave me alone." Her voice is drained, flat. She doesn't move her hands.

"But I—"

"Please."

"Okay," I say, backing up. "Okay," I repeat, hoping she'll

relent and put down her hands and tell me to come back, we can cry on each other's shoulders, we're still friends. That I'm not alone in the world.

But she doesn't.

I head blindly toward my locker. My stomach rumbles, and I think maybe I can get some peanut-butter crackers or something out of one of the vending machines, to make it through the afternoon. I'm not used to skipping lunch, and even though my life is falling apart around me, my practical stomach goes on wanting food, goes on about the business of keeping me alive. I don't know whether to find that comforting and hopeful, or horrifyingly selfish.

Vanessa—and now Sylvie—would vote for selfish, I'm sure.

I touch the necklace Sylvie gave me, as if its stone and metal could ensure that our friendship is still real, still solid. But I can't ignore the truth of what she said to me. It's as if I've had binoculars trained on my own toes, watching only the tiny circle of earth around me, and she has swung them over to show me her world. It's as if I haven't realized until now that there is any other world. I'm so used to seeing myself as the outcast and everyone else as secure and perfect inside their circles of belonging, immune to hurt.

Guilt and shame swirl around in my stomach. I feel small enough to crawl into the locker vents next to me. I try to absorb the fact that I've lost Nick and Sylvie in the same day, and that it's all my fault. I can't even grasp the enormity of this loss, this pain.

As the bell rings to end lunch, I turn the corner into the last hall.

Kids pour out of the cafeteria. I trip over my own feet as Nick and Vanessa emerge together.

They walk down the hall with their backs to me. They're not touching, but they are together, talking. Nick nods at something Vanessa says. They keep walking, away from me.

I drag myself to French class, knowing Vanessa will be there. She bumps my chair on the way to her desk.

Oh, that's original, I say to myself. She should ask Raleigh Barringer for pointers on how to be truly ruthless. Bumping chairs is amateur stuff.

And yet, she still gets to me. When I have to answer a question, I stammer, just because she's in the room. I don't usually make many mistakes, but under her acidic glare, I second-guess my pronunciation of every word. It's not anything she does, it's worrying about what she *might* do. A film of sweat covers my skin by the time my turn ends. I might as well be hauling myself up Crystal Mountain all over again.

The teacher moves on to the next student, and I exhale. I can't bring myself to meet Vanessa's eyes.

🍃 🍃 🍃

Bio is next, with Adriana.

Perfect.

I sit beside her as if she's a shock-sensitive explosive that the slightest whisper might trigger. I can't help wondering if she has noticed Vanessa's new hatred of me, if she'll be drawn to it the way she was drawn to Raleigh's campaign. But Adriana simply lines up her colored pencils, ready to draw the cells we'll be studying today.

She uses the microscope first. "I think that's in focus," she says, and sits back to let me look. My shaking hand touches the knob, and everything blurs.

"Oh, sorry," I say, twisting the knobs, trying to refocus. I'm not sure which way to go, and the blurry white sea under the lens refuses to come clear.

"Let me try," Adriana says. She doesn't snap at me, as I might have expected. On the other side of the room, somebody drops a notebook, and I jump.

And then—I can't believe it. Vanessa is in the hall, right outside the door, glaring at me. She holds a pass in one hand, so she's legit, and she's obviously in no hurry. Our teacher hasn't seen her.

"What's with her?" Adriana asks, breaking away from the microscope for a minute.

I force my eyes back to our bench. "I don't know."

"She looks pissed."

"Well, she—thinks I tried to get between her and Nick."

I still feel Vanessa's eyes burning into my neck, but when

I sneak a glance, she's gone. It doesn't matter. She may not be standing there now, but I know I'll see her again. And again— and again—

Adriana frowns. "Didn't they break up?"

"Yeah, pretty much, but . . ."

"What does she think, she owns him forever? She needs to get over it." Adriana adjusts the focus. "There. Try that."

I do, this time keeping my hands at my sides. I can see the cells now, and I fumble for my pencil.

"Besides, everyone knows you and Nick have always been like *that*." I don't look away from the cells, but I imagine she's twining her fingers together. "In fact, until he started going with Vanessa, I kind of thought he was your boyfriend."

I can't believe she's taking my side in this. "He wasn't. We never—" But of course, we did. "I mean, something did happen between us before Vanessa was around, but—well, it's complicated. And now it looks like they're getting back together. But she's mad at me."

"She'll get over it. If she's smart, she'll concentrate on her own life instead of worrying about you. Attacking other people—it's kind of pathetic when you think about it."

I lift my chin, startled. Astonished she could say that, considering she spent junior high shadowing Raleigh in her mission to crush me. Adriana's face flushes, and she doesn't quite meet my eyes. "I mean, sometimes people get carried away," she says. "They don't think about what they're doing."

"Is that how it is?"

"Yeah. Whether it's revenge, like with Vanessa, or whether it just seems fun. Sometimes people don't get how mean it is until they look back at it later."

Adriana and I have never talked about the horrible things she said to me in junior high, the things Raleigh did that she laughed at, copied, joined in on. I've been too embarrassed to bring it up—what am I going to say, *Remember how you humiliated me?*—but this is the first time I've realized *she* might be embarrassed.

I doubt she will ever apologize to me. But suddenly I'm remembering Adriana as she was in junior high. Her mouth stretched with laughter, her eyes gleaming—yes, I remember that. But I also remember her tagging after Raleigh, hurrying to match Raleigh's pace. The doubt in Adriana's eyes as the two of them leaned against the wall. Her too-loud fake laughter. Even then, as socially incompetent as I was, I sensed the falseness in Adriana's act. Sometimes it was too thin, and the light shone right through it.

Not that she was some helpless pawn. She didn't have a gun pointed at her head. She made choices, and she picked Raleigh for a friend. There were plenty of times when her giggles at my expense were as spontaneous as Raleigh's. But I've never thought until now that she might regret any of it—that maybe some of those giggles have left a sour aftertaste.

Adriana takes her turn at the microscope. I try to make my cell pictures look more like cells and less like squashed octopi.

But my mind is a tangle: Vanessa, Adriana, me. None of us perfect, none of us completely sure of ourselves.

At last, this day is over. I'm in front of my locker, trying to fit all my books into my pack, when Raleigh Barringer laughs somewhere down the hall. Her screech runs through me, triggering every nerve. My head jerks up to track her position.

Oh no. She's talking to Vanessa.

I bow my head and crouch over my pack, fumbling with the zipper. A Raleigh-Vanessa alliance would finish me off. That's all I need: Vanessa's anger joined with Raleigh's viciousness.

Tears gather in my throat, but I swallow them down. I didn't cry in the halls of junior high. I'm not going to break now.

My pack refuses to close. I pull the fabric tighter, yank on the zipper, anxious to escape. Why do zippers always stick when you have somewhere to go?

Suddenly, I realize that I don't even know how I'm getting home. I haven't seen Nick since this morning, before he and Vanessa had their talk. He never answered my text.

The knot in my throat hardens, a crushing pressure. I can't take any more of this. I'll suffocate or else I'll—

Whack! Something smacks my back, and a shadow swoops overhead. Instinctively, I duck even lower.

Raleigh Barringer hops on one leg, adjusting her balance. It's clear she has just tripped over me.

"What the hell?!" she says. "God, Maggie, what are you doing in the middle of the hall?"

Sure, blame me, I think. Even though I'm not in the middle of the hall at all, but right in front of the lockers. If I were any farther over, I'd be *inside* them. Which would probably be just fine with her.

I am sick of Raleigh. So very, very sick.

I've.

Had.

Enough.

Dry-mouthed, I say, "You should watch where you're going."

Her eyebrows rise. "*What* did you say to me?"

I stand, scraping up the determination that took me to the summit of Crystal. No matter what happens now, it's not going to happen with me crouched below her in groveling position. "I said, you should watch where you're going."

With a roll of her eyes, she turns away. "You're the one who should watch out."

All the pain she has caused me concentrates in my gut, crystallizes in this moment. I take a step after her, boiling.

"*Excuse* me?" I bellow. "What was that?"

I'm thinking—if I'm thinking at all—*Enough*. I can't go back to being the girl Raleigh kicks around.

She whirls to face me. "Don't talk to me like that."

"I'll talk to you any way I want. Do you think you own me?"

"*Own* you?! What are you talking about? You got in my way and tripped me, and I snapped at you. Get over it."

Rage swells inside me until I think my eyeballs are going to pop out. The top of my skull threatens to shoot toward the ceiling.

Raleigh.

It's her fault I don't fit in. She's the reason I can't relate to anyone like a normal person. She's why I screw up all my relationships. Because of her, I never learned how to be anything but a victim.

If she hadn't been around, I would've learned how to relate to people. How to respond to Nick when he first kissed me. How to listen to Sylvie. How to have friends and be a friend.

"I'm sick of you," I snarl. "The way you scream at me. I'm sick of you kicking me, and texting about me, and calling me names, and telling me I should kill myself. Don't you *ever* say a word about me again!"

The halls are mostly empty by now, and my voice bounces off the lockers, echoing. A few kids on their way to sports practice or detention pause and turn their heads.

She gapes at me. And then she says, her voice dripping icicles, "Grow up, Maggie. You're talking about things that happened *years* ago. What are you, stuck in junior high?"

If I've ever had any fantasy that I could squash Raleigh, make her sorry, it's dissolving now. Because that sentence is the worst. It penetrates like acid, right to my bones. "What are you, stuck in junior high?"

Yes. Yes, I am.

I think I always will be.

twenty-nine

Time stops.

A few people have gathered. Some of Raleigh's friends are waiting for her. Vanessa, who had turned away after talking to Raleigh, has now turned back, watching us. I know who she's rooting for. But—I have to hold back a gulp—Nick has joined her. And Luis.

About a dozen people watch us, like the rings of spectators that used to form in seventh and eighth grades whenever Raleigh would torment me.

And then I remember I'm not completely helpless against her. I do have one weapon, thanks to Adriana.

"Junior high?" I begin. "You wouldn't have even made it *out* of junior high, if . . ."

Her eyes flash; she tenses. The others bend forward a little. I catch Nick's eye. Of everyone watching, he's the only one who knows what I'm talking about.

The words are in my mouth, ready. I want to crack Raleigh's smooth, contemptuous, superior face, with its veneer of world travel and Italian chic. I want to see her crumble. It's a black tide in me, and I remember this surge of energy so well from junior high, because I had it every day back then.

Stuck in junior high.

Stuck.

It occurs to me that this is the first real exchange I've had with Raleigh since she got back. For more than a month now, I've worried about her plotting against me, picking up where she left off. But the truth is that she's barely wasted a thought on me.

I'm the one who's been carrying the whole burden of seventh and eighth grades.

Raleigh waits, her eyes narrowing, but I don't say what I'd planned to. I don't bring up her eighth-grade crimes, her suffering at the hands of Scott Brewer.

It's old news.

It's pathetic.

It will never give me back what I've lost.

All I say is, "Go to hell, Raleigh."

She sneers. "Great comeback." She turns and stalks off with her friends while I stand there, willing my legs to keep holding me up.

🍃   🍃   🍃

I stare at my backpack, my open locker, a pen that fell from my bag when Raleigh tripped over me. I don't know what to do with any of them. I sit on the floor. I pick up the pen, put it down, pick up the backpack.

I start to unzip the pocket where I usually keep my knife, wanting to squeeze it. I need something to remind me I'm not the little girl Raleigh once picked on and stomped all over. I've climbed Crystal Mountain.

"What's wrong?"

Luis stands over me. I'm still sitting with my back pressed against the lockers. I look up, but I can't find my voice.

"What was that about?" he says.

I shake my head and stagger to my feet.

Pen inside pack. Forget about zipping it. Hold pack. Close locker.

"You okay, Maggie?" Luis asks.

Nick is here, too, now, hovering silently. Vanessa's gone. I don't know where she went.

There's a strange buzzing in my head. I have to get home, home to the couch or the piano or the wood shop or my bed. Somewhere safe. Somewhere that is not here.

"Come on," Luis says, taking my backpack.

Apparently, they are giving me a ride.

I stumble out to the parking lot with them. I'm made of glass. I might crack into pieces before I can make it to the car.

"Why are you being so nice to me?" I ask Luis.

He gives me a strange look. As if to say, *Why wouldn't I?* I've always thought of Luis more as Nick's friend than mine. I've assumed he wouldn't talk to me if we weren't thrown together in Nick's car every day. But here he is carrying my backpack, patting my arm, guiding me to the car as if I'm a hundred and fifty years old.

I get in the backseat.

"How're you doing, Maggie?" Luis asks.

I always thought that confronting Raleigh would be my triumph. She would collapse, sobbing and pleading. She would learn how horrible it was to take what she'd dished out.

But I'm—empty. And of course, it didn't turn out the way I planned. Raleigh is still Raleigh.

"You want to talk about it?" Nick says, speaking to me for the first time this afternoon.

"No."

"Okay."

They accept my silence, all the way to Luis's house.

Luis pats my shoulder when I take his place in the front seat. I say thanks and settle in beside Nick.

I have no idea what to say. Automatically, my hand seeks the knife in my backpack, to squeeze the cool metal, but it's not there.

My stomach lurches.

I search every inch of the pouch, and then I try to remember the last time I saw it. I'm sure I had it with me on the mountain, but it's definitely not here.

"What are you looking for?" Nick asks.

"My knife. I think I lost it." It hasn't even been two months since he bought it for me. I can't look him in the face.

But all he says is, "Oh."

"I can't believe I lost it! I must've dropped it on Crystal."

"It's okay. You can borrow mine, like you used to."

"That's not the point."

We drive in silence for another minute before he says, "What's the matter? I thought you'd be happy you got a chance to stand up to Raleigh."

"A lot of good it did me. She still tore me apart." I turn my head to the window, though nothing that flashes by registers.

"No, she didn't." He laughs softly. "Nobody ever talks back to her. Did you see the look on her face?"

I sigh. Now that Raleigh and I have escalated to screaming at each other, is it going to be open warfare with her again? We Hate Maggie, the high school version? "I'm so tired of being scared."

"Uh—you, scared? I've seen you face rattlesnakes and wind-storms."

Those are easy things, compared to dealing with people. I would rather face the worst a mountain can throw at me than spend five minutes with Raleigh Barringer.

"Do you remember that day you first showed me your mushroom book?" he says.

"Yes."

"That was the first time I thought, 'Damn, this girl is *something.*' I mean, I knew you weren't going to poison anyone. But you had this whole world of your own, you knew all this stuff, and it was obvious those other girls were wrong about you."

"That's what you thought?" I say. "That *they* were wrong?"

"Well, yeah. And you're still like that. You don't copy the other girls at school. You have your own life."

I'm trying to digest this view of myself when he says, "I wish I could do that with my dad. Tell him to go to hell, even if it's just in my own mind."

"Your dad?! Nick, we talked about this. He judges you by how much biochemistry you know. Which is crazy."

"Not just biochemistry," he says. "History, and math, and—"

"Oh, Nick. Stop it."

He adjusts the side mirror, pushing the knob to move it toward the car, then pushing it back.

"Your dad's a miserable person. He's got plenty of faults of his own. You heard him in the lab—he made a mistake right in front of us and wouldn't admit it." I wish Nick would look at me. "So how can you believe anything he says about you?"

Nick laughs, but not as if he really thinks anything is funny. I want to shake him. Just because his father *acts* like

Nick isn't good enough, why does he buy into that? Why does he let someone else's opinion rule him that way? He ought to know—

Oh.

The truth breaks over me like a wave. I know what he's thinking because I've fed it to myself. *If I weren't so quiet and skinny and strange, Raleigh and Adriana wouldn't pick on me. If I wore the right clothes, I would fit in. If I knew the right thing to say. If I liked the things everyone else likes, instead of weird things like mushrooms. If I didn't study so much. If I wore makeup, if I knew their songs . . .*

I don't always believe that, but a lot of the time I do. I fall into it without even realizing it.

After all this time, my life still revolves around being Raleigh Barringer's victim. I carry her voice in my head. Even if I had dragged out her dirty laundry today, drawn a few drops of blood, gotten a few moments of revenge, it wouldn't have mattered. Raleigh isn't the problem anymore.

The problem is that I haven't moved on.

Which isn't to say that she has nothing to answer for. She, and Adriana, and Lissa Carpenter, and Ethan Crannick, and all the rest—they were wrong. And maybe their consciences bother them, the way Adriana's did in lab today. Maybe they'll be on the receiving end someday, or they'll look back and cringe at what they did.

Or maybe not. It isn't a question of conquering them, or getting their approval. It isn't about revenge or apologies—it isn't about *them* at all, their power, their opinions. Either way, what they did wasn't my fault, and I don't have to wait any longer for my life to start.

Stuck in fear, stuck in junior high.

Nick pulls up in front of my house, but I don't get out, and he doesn't rush me. We have more to settle between us. He shifts into PARK.

"What happened to Vanessa?" I ask. "I saw you together in the hall before we left school. . . ."

"She went home." No clues in his voice.

"I'm sorry I didn't tell you she wanted to get back together. I should have. It's just—"

"Yeah, you should have," he says.

"Are you going back to her?"

He rubs the steering wheel. Rain begins to spot the windshield. "Maybe. I don't know."

"What about us? Are we—okay?"

"I don't know that, either." He moves the side mirror again. "If I get back together with Vanessa, she doesn't want me spending time with you. She says she doesn't trust us alone."

"She doesn't trust *me*," I say.

He doesn't argue.

"What about you? Do you trust me?"

"I don't know." He hesitates. "On the trails, I do. There's nobody I trust more on a mountain."

My hand slips into the knife pocket again—but, of course, it's still empty. "If you go back to her, we won't be able to hike together again."

"I know."

The pain seems to split my stomach, chest, throat. I can't imagine this whole part of my life closing off. I can't imagine him giving it up, either. "And that's okay with you?"

"Look," he says, his eyes on the dashboard, not on me. "Maybe Vanessa and I don't have as much in common, but things aren't complicated with her. She says what she wants. With you, it's like—I'm all over the place. I don't know what you want. I'm not sure *you* know what you want."

What do I want?

I want to be beautiful, happy, loved. I want to feel like I belong in this world. I want to feel like I'm good enough to have all that.

Something rings a bell in my mind when I think that. Something about being good enough. Because hasn't Nick just sat here and told me that *he's* not good enough for his father?

What happens if I believe—or even pretend to believe—that I'm good enough?

What if I can finally say the right thing to Nick at the right time?

I breathe in. "I meant what I told you on Crystal. What I want is to hike with you." My voice squeaks, but I keep going. "And talk to you. And watch your stupid basketball games. And kiss you." Waves of embarrassment wash over me, drenching me. I have to unzip my coat. "And it would be nice if I weren't so afraid of saying that to you, and it would be nice if you felt the same way, but that's basically what I want."

I can't bear to be in the car another minute. I burst out of the passenger side, out into a gray drizzle. He says, "Maggie, wait," but I don't. I run to my house.

The door is locked. Dad's not home yet, and Mom must have an afternoon shift. I fumble with my key, and then Nick is there on the step with me.

"Maggie."

"If you're going to give a nice little speech about how you like me but just not that way, or how I had my chance the day we climbed Eagle but it's too late now, or how you've decided Vanessa is your soul mate after all . . . that's okay, we can skip it." The key finally turns.

He follows me in. As usual, the living room is as dark as a closet.

"Do you want me to say anything here, or do you just want to keep doing all the talking yourself?" he asks.

When I don't answer, he puts his hands on my shoulders and turns me to face him. I can't meet his eyes.

"Maggie." But instead of saying more, he wraps his arms around me.

I bury my face in his shirt.

"Your heart's beating," I say. Maybe the most senseless piece of conversation ever, but it's all I can think of: the rhythm beneath my ear.

"Good to know."

I lift my head up. He brushes his lips against mine as if I might break under his touch.

"Don't do this unless you mean it," I say.

He kisses me again. The kiss deepens, his mouth hot, his tongue meeting mine. We press into each other. He kisses me until the room is whirling, until it hurts to stop.

thirty

After my mother comes home and Nick leaves, I go upstairs to call Sylvie. I've texted her a couple of times this after-noon, telling her that I'm sorry, that I care about her, that I'm ready to listen. But I want to talk to her—and most of all, to give her a chance to speak.

I'm prepared to leave another apology on her voice mail if she doesn't take my call, but she picks up. "How are you doing?" I say.

"Not great."

"Sylvie, I'm sorry I didn't listen to you more about Wendy. You're right; I haven't been there for you. I knew you were having some trouble, but I figured everything would turn out okay for you. I should've—"

"Why did you think that?"

Because I always assume everything turns out okay for everyone but me. I don't say this to Sylvie, but it's a shock to realize this is exactly how I see the world. Which means I go around thinking, *You're fine. You're not me, so you will get what you want.* Only now am I starting to question this, to see how screwed-up and untrue it is. "I guess because you're always on top of things . . . but I'm sorry I didn't take your problems seriously. Do you want to talk about it?"

"Are you sure you want to hear it?"

"Of course. I know how much Wendy meant to you."

Sylvie sobs. Then she gathers herself enough to say, "She said it's too hard trying to be with someone who's still in high school. That she's taking courses in government and politics and philosophy, while I'm still hung up on 'baby' things like the high school yearbook."

"That's so unfair."

"She said she's meeting so many new people and discovering so many new ideas that she doesn't want to be 'stuck' with one person right now. She wants to travel. I'm not growing up fast enough for her, or something."

"Uck."

"And the worst thing is, she kept saying, 'No offense,' before everything. Like that made it better. Like it would hurt less just because she put those two words in front."

I listen, offering sympathy where I can. I have no magical advice but I realize, as she goes on, that this is the most I've let her say in a long time. Maybe that's worth more than any philosophical speeches I could come up with. I listen until she's talked out.

"Thank you, Maggie," she says before we hang up.

"Any time."

On Tuesday, I wake up with an enormous zit on my nose. My hair decides to puff out on one side of my head and lie greasily flat on the other. When I walk down the school hall, I'm suddenly self-conscious about my shirt. I bought it at a thrift store, and its colors thrilled me—shades of violet that melt into one another like a watercolor—but nobody else has a shirt anything like it.

I'm not sure about these shoes, either.

I remind myself that Sylvie told me bright colors look good on me, especially blue and purple. And I remember seeing it myself, in the dressing-room mirror on a shopping trip with her. Even if all I can see today is the zit and the crazy hair.

At lunch, Sylvie and Nick have to go to a student council meeting. I sit alone with a book, trying to ignore the girls giggling at the table behind me. I can't hear what they're whispering about, but my mind supplies the script: *Have you ever seen a huger, redder zit than the one on Maggie's face? And what's with that shirt? How can Nick Cleary stand to kiss her without gagging? Vanessa says he knows how to kiss—why's he wasting his time with Maggie Camden? She washes her hair in the toilet, remember?*

At practically every table in this cafeteria, there's someone who laughed at me in junior high, who shoved me or tripped me, who forwarded those texts and contributed to the We Hate Maggie sites.

Most of them have forgotten by now.

The girls at the table behind me could be laughing about anything. I assume it's about me because I always assume it's about me. Because once upon a time, it was.

But we're not in junior high anymore.

Not everyone is intent on hunting me down.

Raleigh Barringer floats into the room and heads for her usual table. She hasn't reactivated her troops against me, and I don't believe she's going to. Is it because I stood up to her, as Nick said? Or is it just that we're older now? I stare at her and when she looks my way, for the first time ever, I don't need to drop my eyes.

Vanessa's at her old table, ignoring me. Nick called her last night to tell her he didn't want to get back together. When I told him I was afraid she was gearing up for war with me, he said no. That no matter how angry she was yesterday, she has too much pride to start a public feud.

But even though he knows Vanessa better than I do, and even though I always did respect her more than Raleigh Barringer, I'm not so sure.

All of which makes the apology I owe Vanessa even harder to deliver.

I'd love to hide under my table instead, but I want to get this over with. Especially after the scene with Sylvie yesterday,

I never again want to assume I'm the only perso
lems, the only one who gets hurt.

I rise on shaky legs and cross to Vanessa.

"What?" she says. Her voice is cold and hard as steel, but I would swear I see a flash of fear in her eyes. Does she think I'm going to gloat about Nick? Does she actually believe I have that in me?

"I wanted to tell you I'm sorry." I wish I could calm my quavering voice, but I plunge ahead. "I should've been honest with you and Nick. And I never meant for you to get hurt when—"

"I'm fine." Her words rush over mine; her eyes narrow. "Don't feel sorry for me."

"I wasn't, I didn't mean that, it's only that I—"

"Maggie, stop it. If you don't mind . . ." She flaps a hand, dismissing me. "I'd like to get on with my life. Which doesn't include you."

I flee back to my own table, trembling so badly I can barely hold my book. I would rather grind tinfoil between my teeth than go through that again. But at least I've said what needed to be said.

My phone vibrates with a message from Nick, who's still in his student council meeting. **I'm dying of boredom. Class treasurer being grilled over 5-cent mistake. Let's go back to Crystal.**

Okay with me, I type back. I need to find my knife anyway.

What's with you and that knife? You seem overly attached to it.

I really like the guy who gave it to me.

There's a pause. Then: He's not so great. I hear he doesn't even know how proteins fold.

I answer: That doesn't bother me. I don't know how proteins fold, either.

The bell rings. Nobody rushes to walk with me, but that's okay. I join the crowd of kids streaming into the hall without shrinking away from them, without trying to make myself invisible. As if I have a right to be here.

ACKNOWLEDGMENTS

Many people have helped me bring this book to life, and have done so with warmth and wisdom. Thank you to everyone at Curtis Brown Ltd., especially Ginger Knowlton, and to the crew at Penguin, especially Leila Sales and Regina Hayes, for their hard work, insight, and encouragement.

I appreciate the writer friends who critiqued drafts of this book (Martha Cooney, Jessica Dimuzio, Colleen Rowan Kosinski, and Ilene Wong), and those who talked me through the ups and downs (Michelle Davidson Argyle, Lisa Brackmann, Nathan Bransford, Megan Crewe, Angela De Groot, Kelly Fineman, Beth Kephart, and Caragh M. O'Brien). Group hugs go to the Debs, Milestones, Kidlit Authors' Club, 2k classes, and Spinners.

I also thank the readers who have sent messages about what my books mean to them; who have come to my live events, invited me to their book clubs and stores and libraries, or shared my books with others. I treasure each message.

To the family and friends who have continued to support me in pursuing this dream: my sincere and loving thanks for always being there. And to John, my partner on the hiking trails and in life: more gratitude and love than I could ever fit on this page.